OFFICIALLY WITHDRAWN
Jefferson School Library
1400 Ada Street
Berkeley, CA 94702

The Graphic Novel

Rapunzel

retold by Stephanie Peters
illustrated by Jeffrey Stewart Timmins

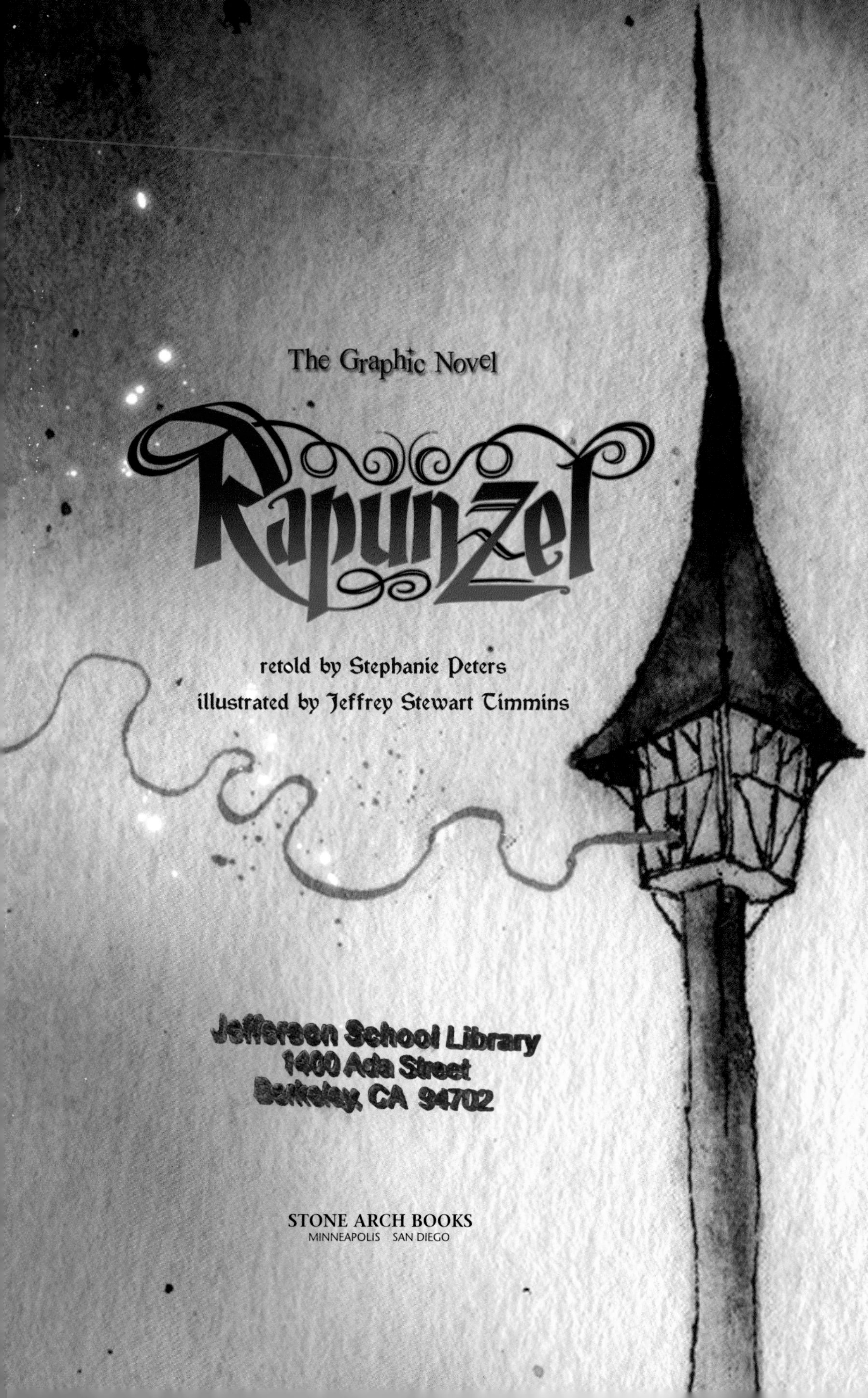

STONE ARCH BOOKS
MINNEAPOLIS SAN DIEGO

Graphic Spin is published by Stone Arch Books,
A Capstone Imprint
1710 Roe Crest Drive
North Mankato, Minnesota 56003
www.capstonepub.com

Library of Congress Cataloging-in-Publication Data
Peters, Stephanie True, 1965–
    Rapunzel / by Stephanie Peters; illustrated by Jeffrey Stewart Timmins.
    p. cm. — (Graphic Spin)
    ISBN 978-1-4342-1194-1 (library binding)
    ISBN 978-1-4342-1392-1 (pbk.)
    1. Graphic novels. [1. Graphic novels. 2. Fairy tales. 3. Folklore–Germany.] I. Timmins, Jeffrey Stewart,
ill. II. Rapunzel. English. III. Title.
PZ7.7.P44Rap 2009
741.5'973–dc22   2008032047

Summary: Long ago, a beautiful maiden named Rapunzel lived a life of loneliness. Taken at birth by an evil
witch, she remained hidden, locked within a giant tower. Then one day, a prince heard her voice through the
forest. To reach her, he must climb Rapunzel's lovely locks and avoid being caught by the witch.

Creative Director: Heather Kindseth
Designer: Bob Lentz

Printed in the United States of America in North Mankato, Minnesota.
112013
007833R

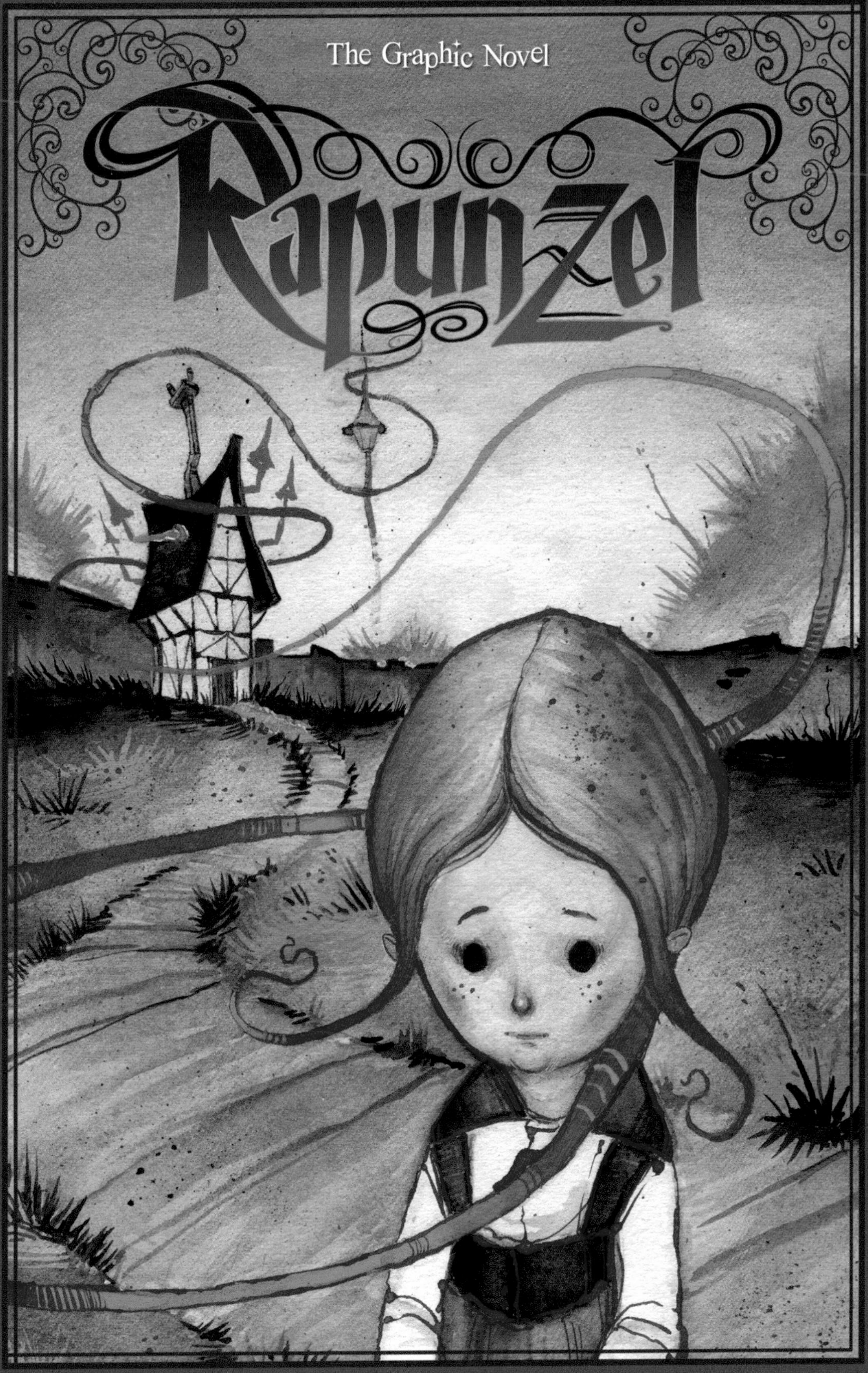
The Graphic Novel
Rapunzel

Cast of Characters

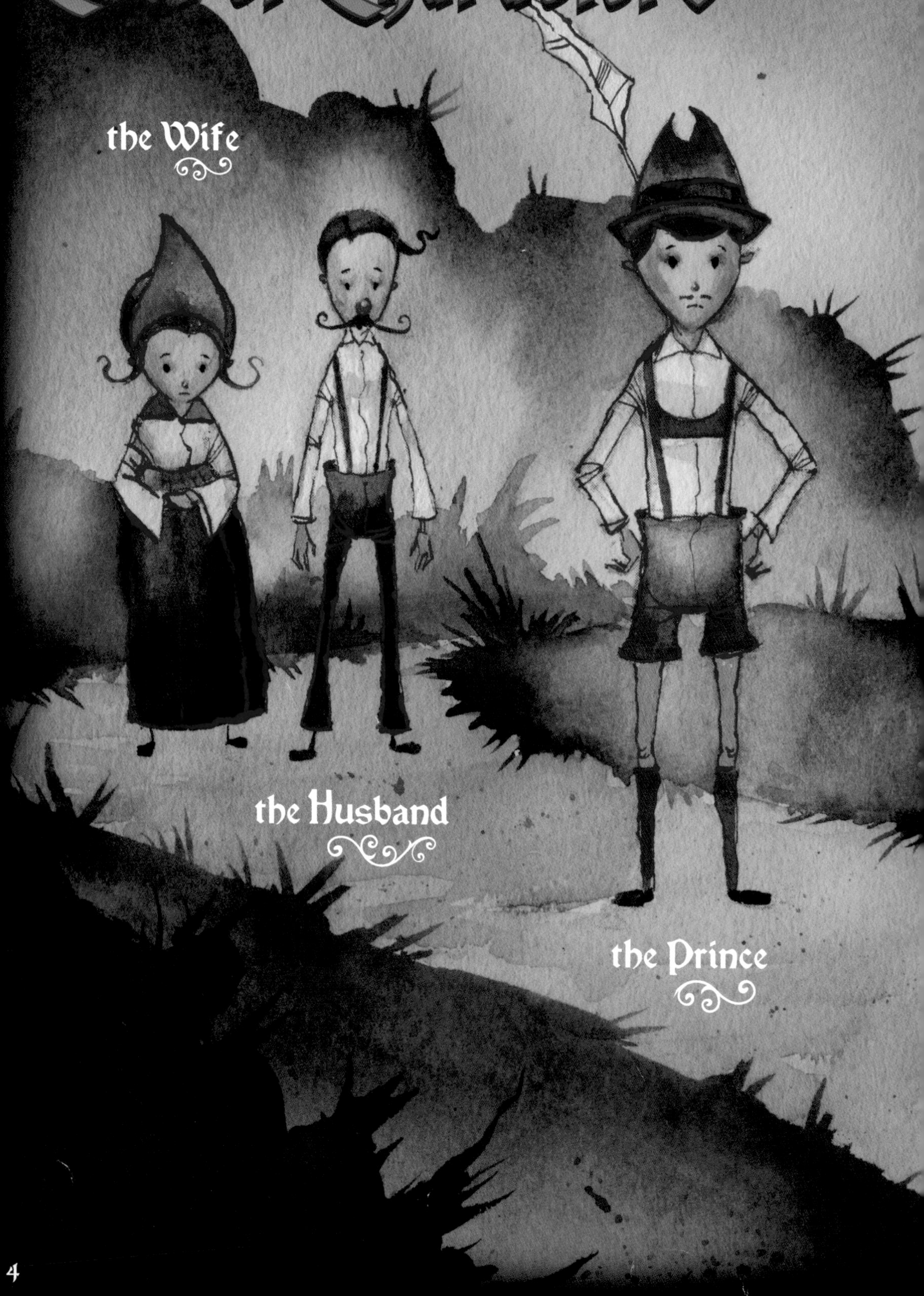

the Wife
the Husband
the Prince

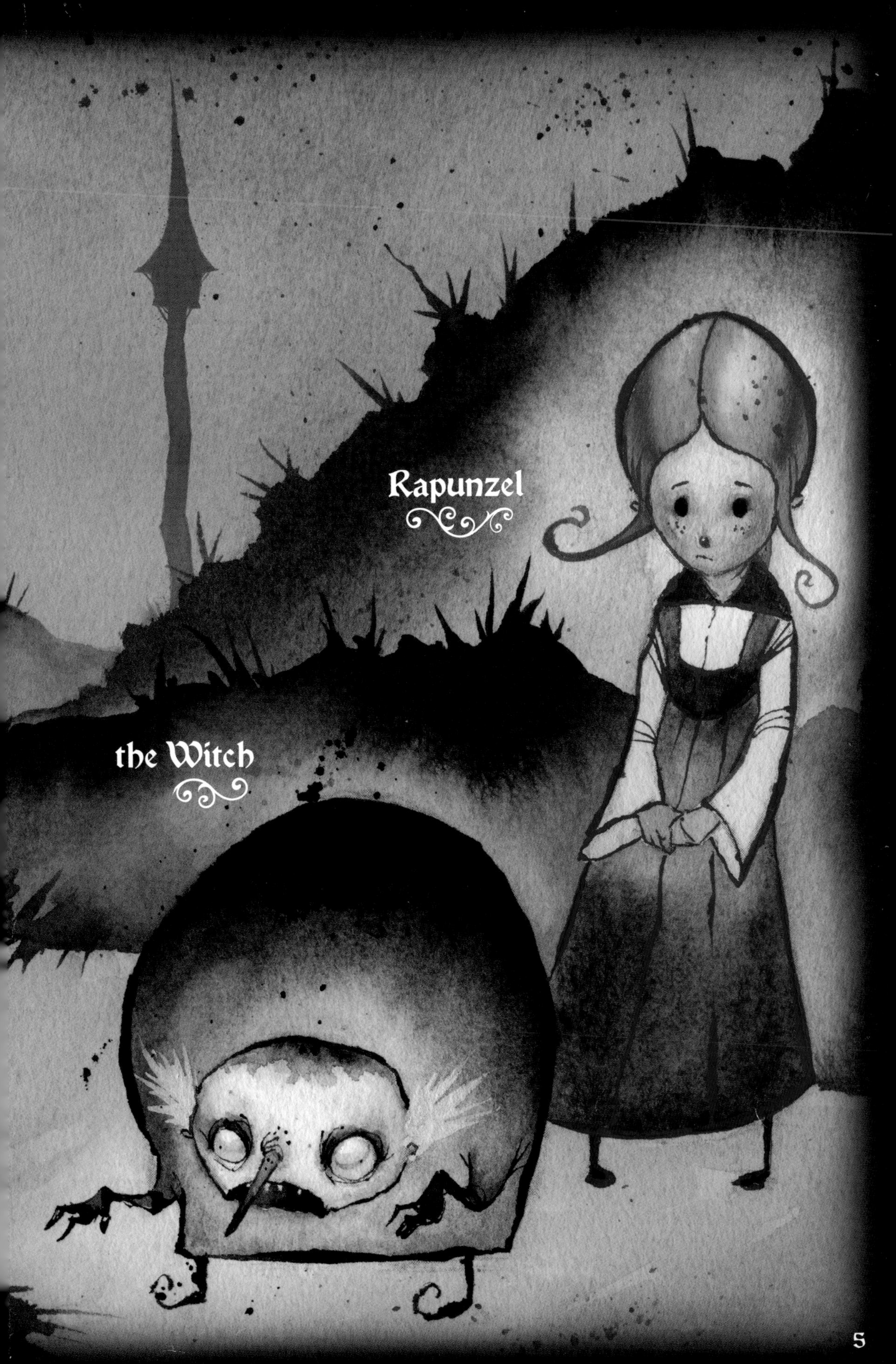
Rapunzel
the Witch

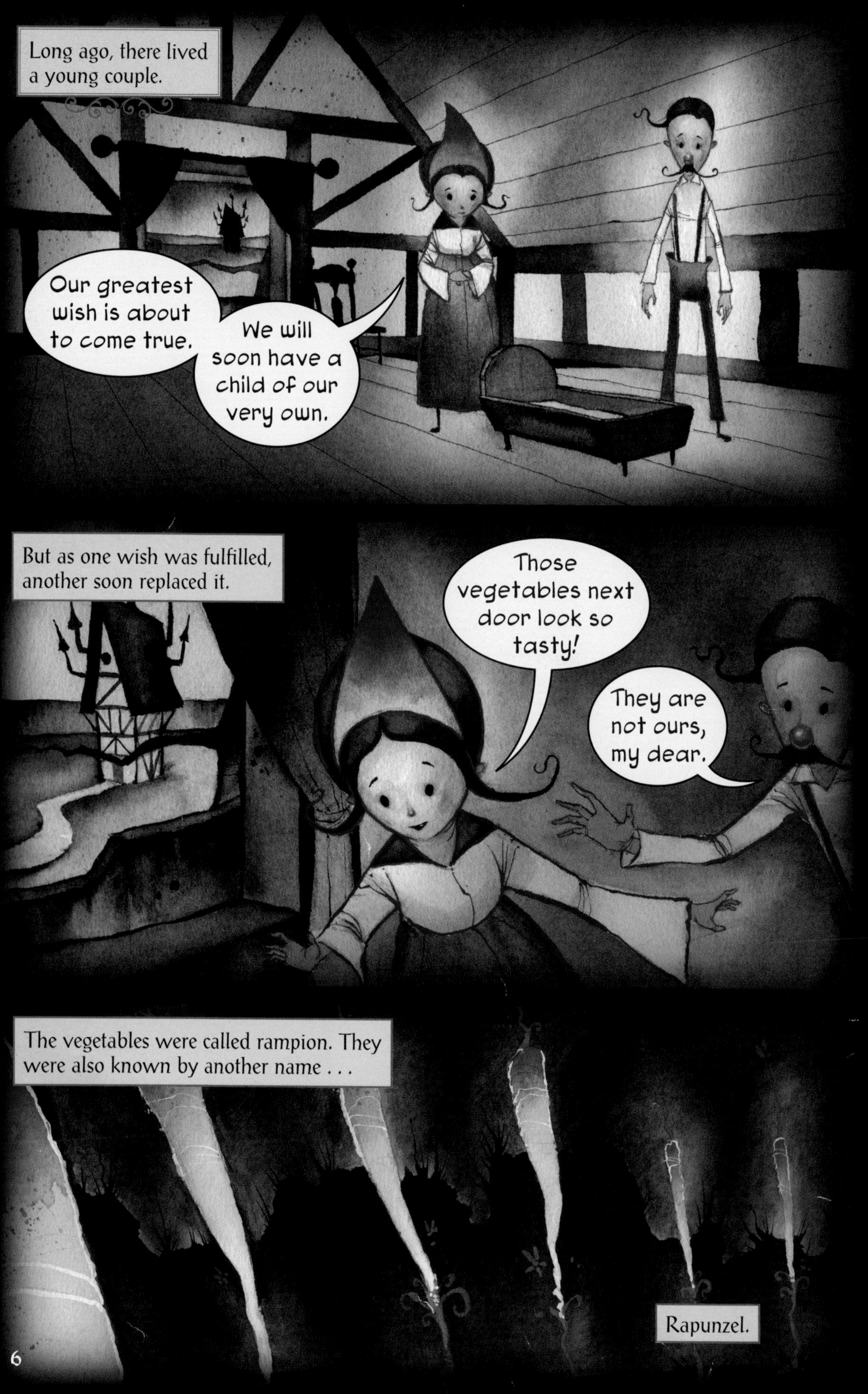
Long ago, there lived a young couple.
Our greatest wish is about to come true.
We will soon have a child of our very own.
But as one wish was fulfilled, another soon replaced it.
Those vegetables next door look so tasty!
They are not ours, my dear.
The vegetables were called rampion. They were also known by another name . . .
Rapunzel.

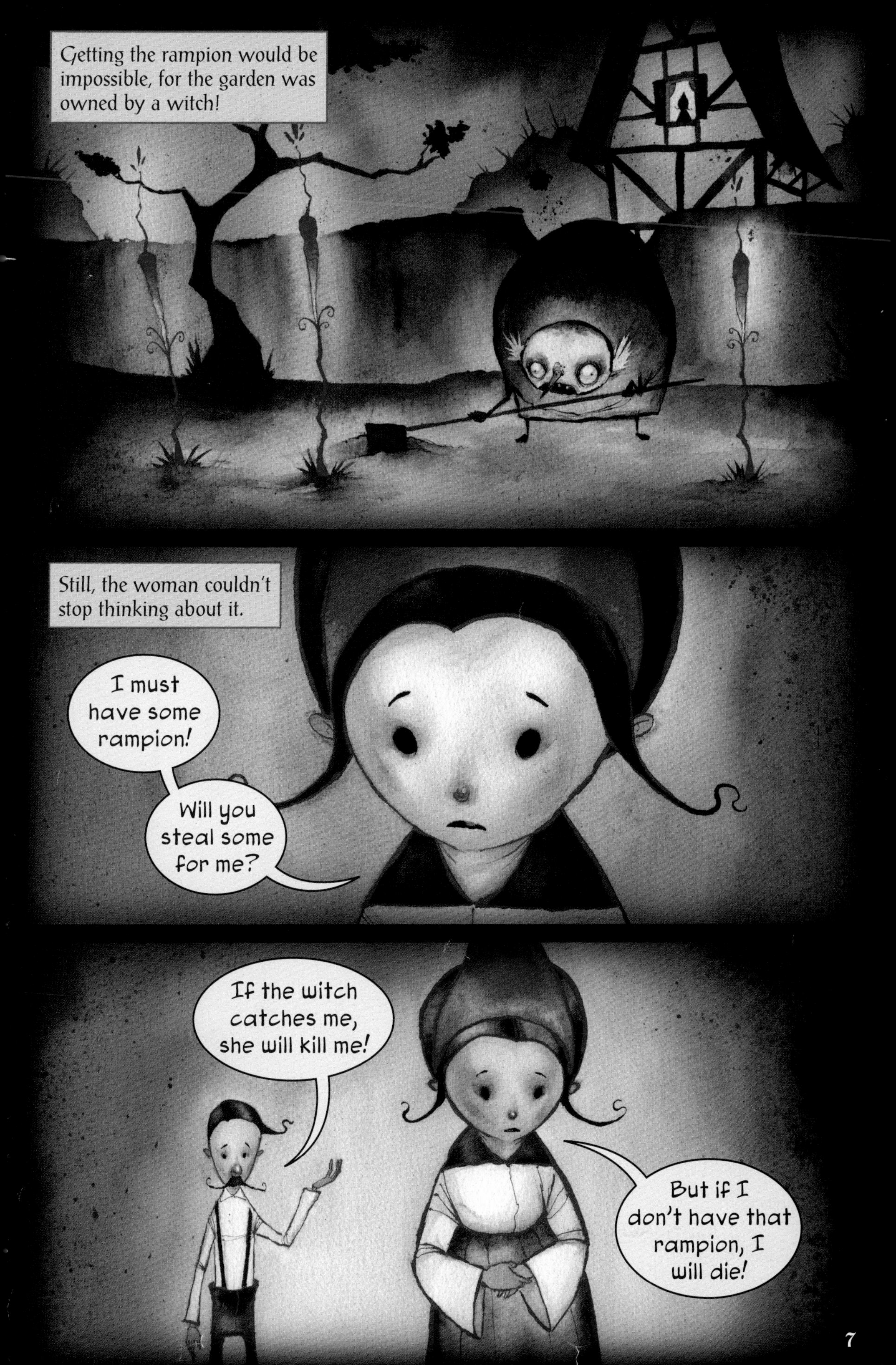
Getting the rampion would be impossible, for the garden was owned by a witch!
Still, the woman couldn't stop thinking about it.
I must have some rampion!
Will you steal some for me?
If the witch catches me, she will kill me!
But if I don't have that rampion, I will die!

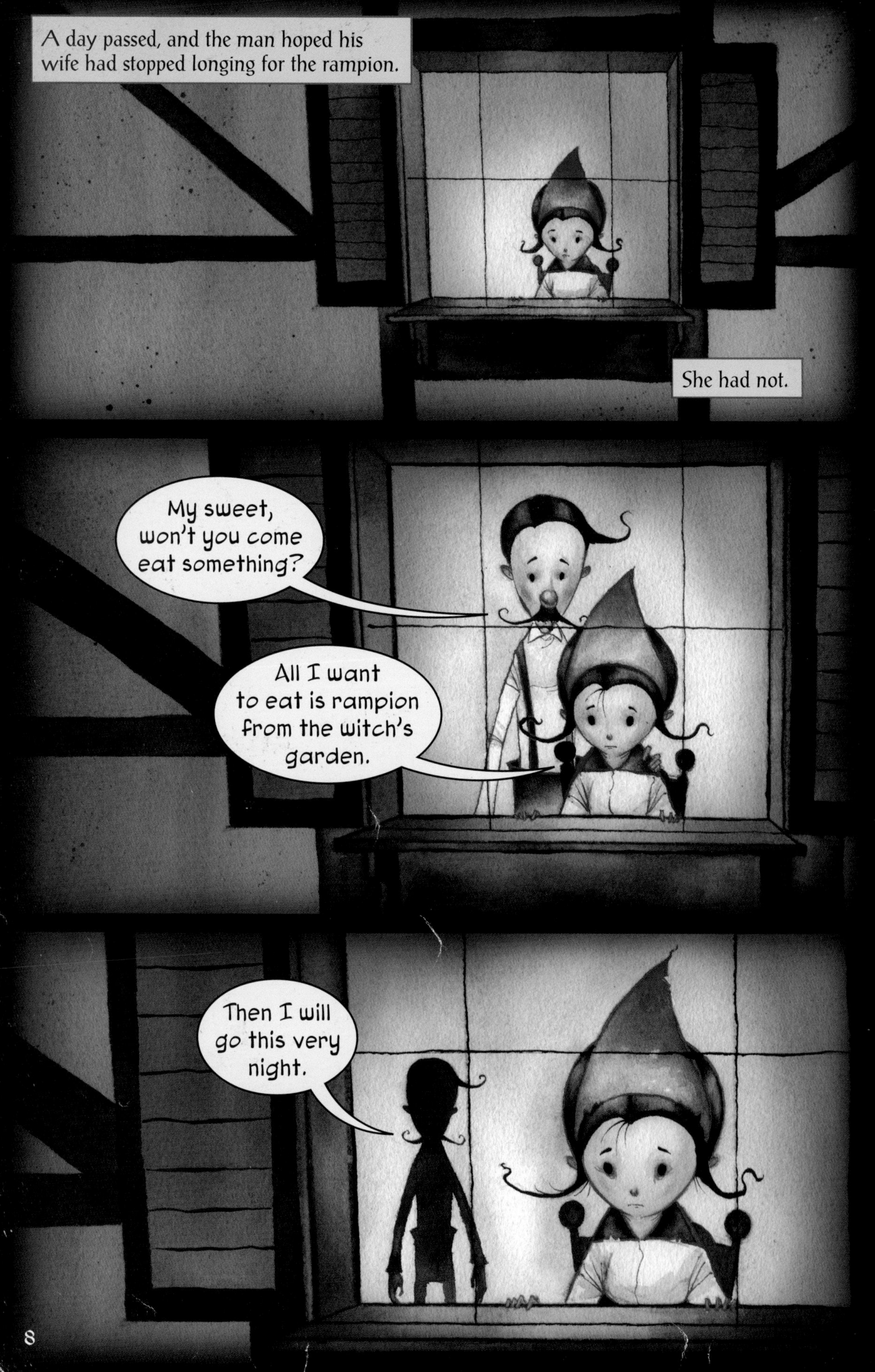
A day passed, and the man hoped his wife had stopped longing for the rampion.
She had not.
My sweet, won't you come eat something?
All I want to eat is rampion from the witch's garden.
Then I will go this very night.

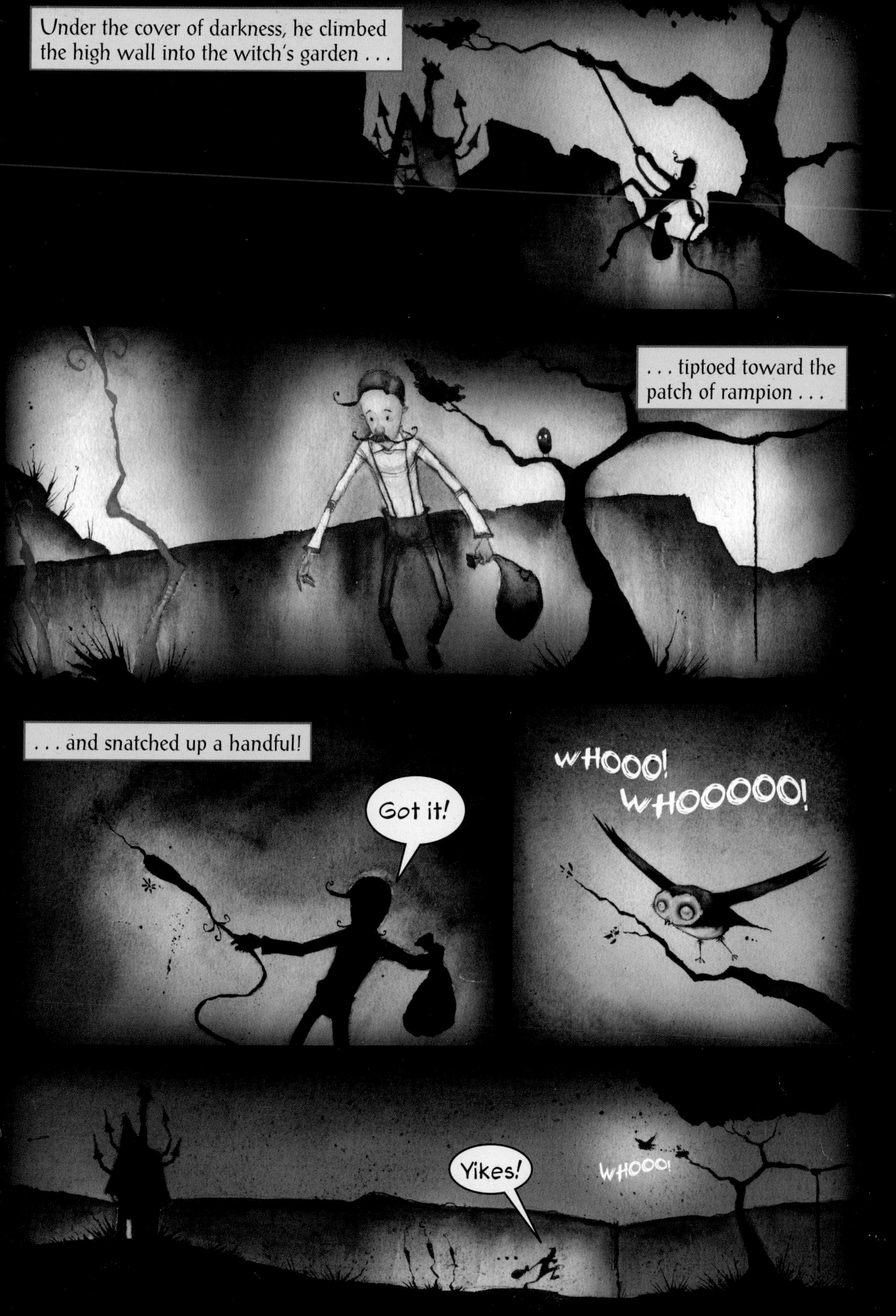
Under the cover of darkness, he climbed the high wall into the witch's garden . . .
. . . tiptoed toward the patch of rampion . . .
. . . and snatched up a handful!
Got it!
WHOOO!
WHOOOOOO!
Yikes!
WHOOO!

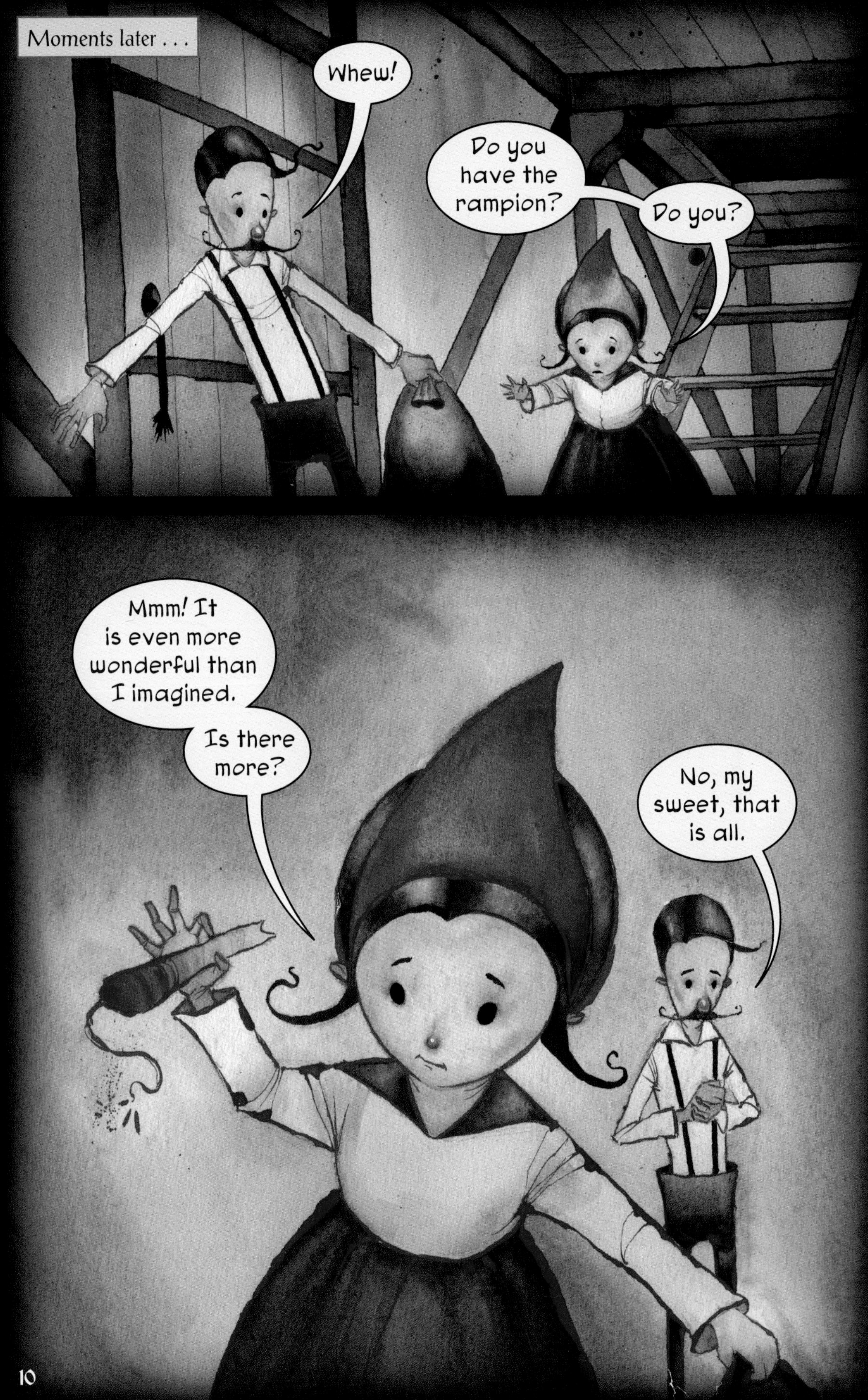
Moments later . . .
Whew!
Do you have the rampion?
Do you?
Mmm! It is even more wonderful than I imagined.
Is there more?
No, my sweet, that is all.

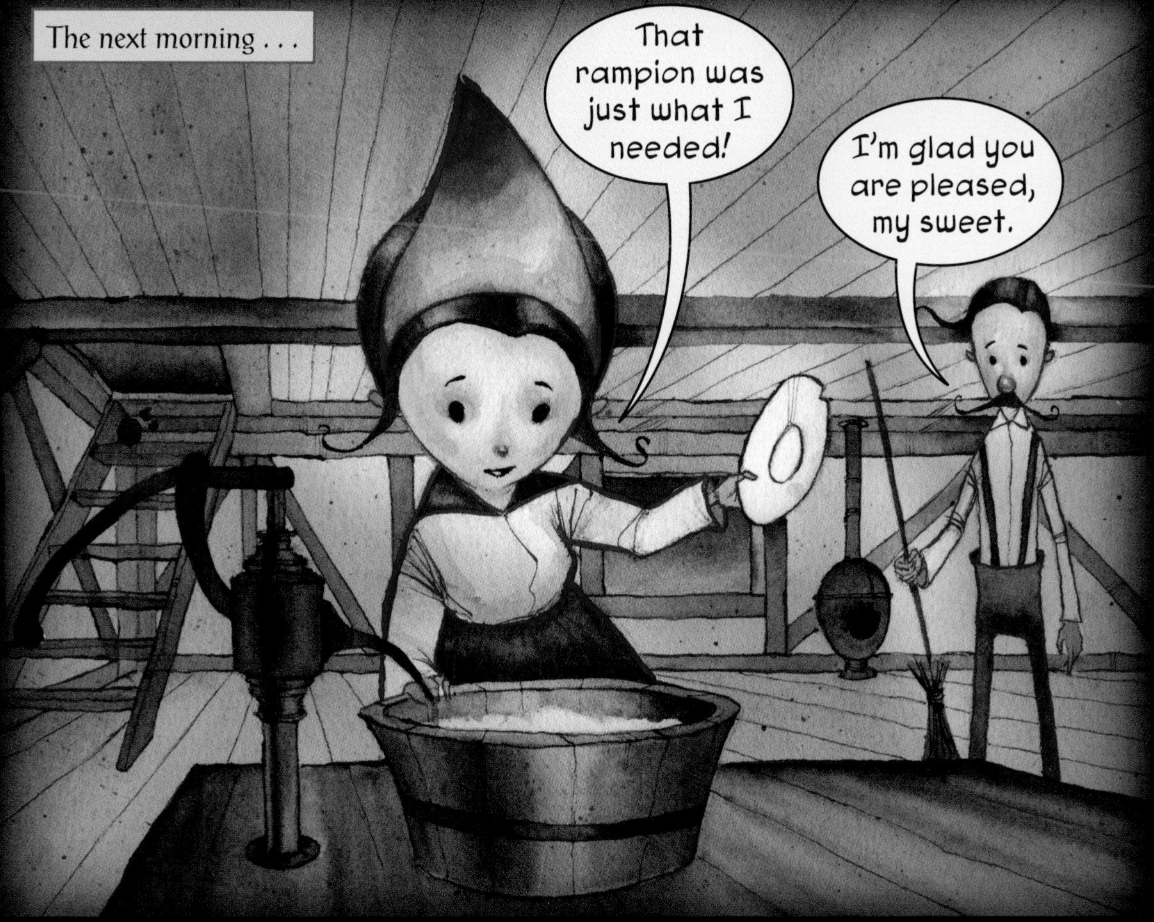
The next morning . . .
That rampion was just what I needed!
I'm glad you are pleased, my sweet.

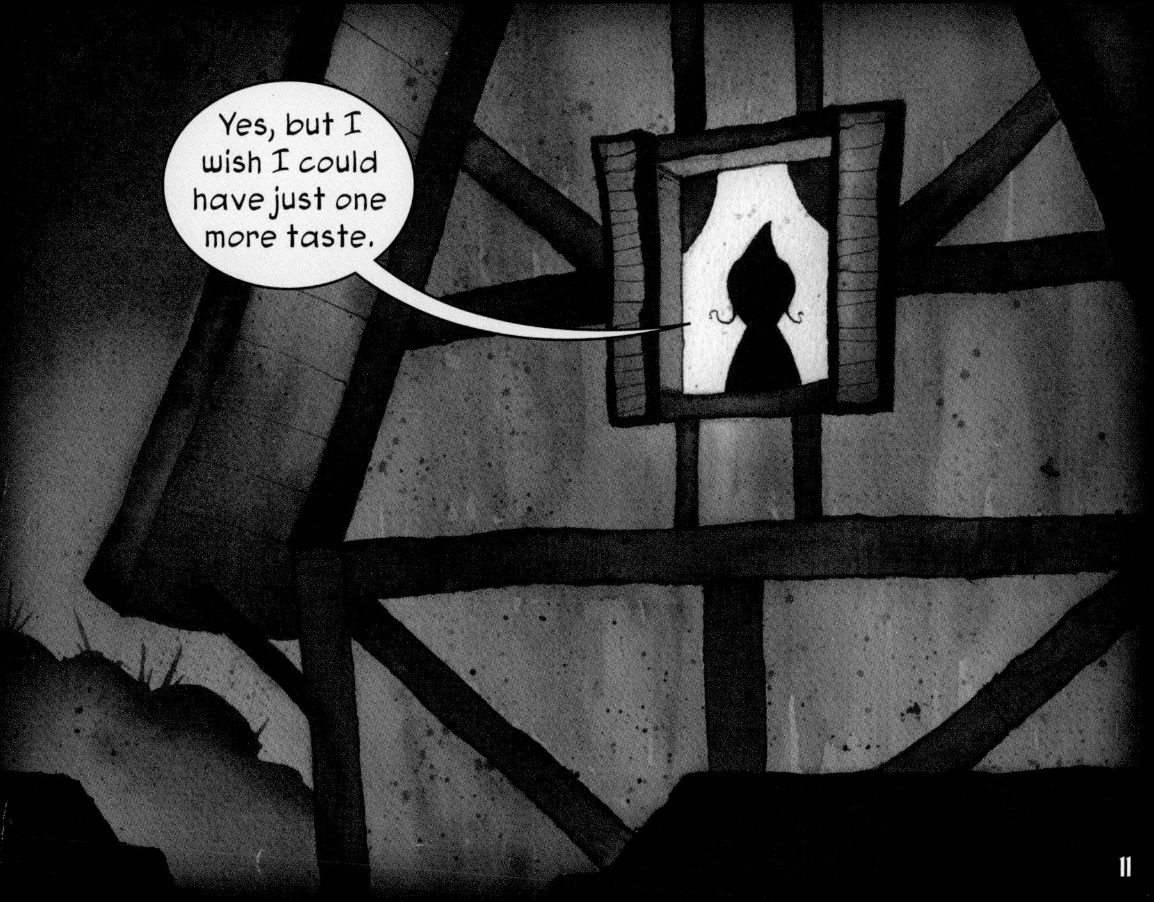
Yes, but I wish I could have just one more taste.

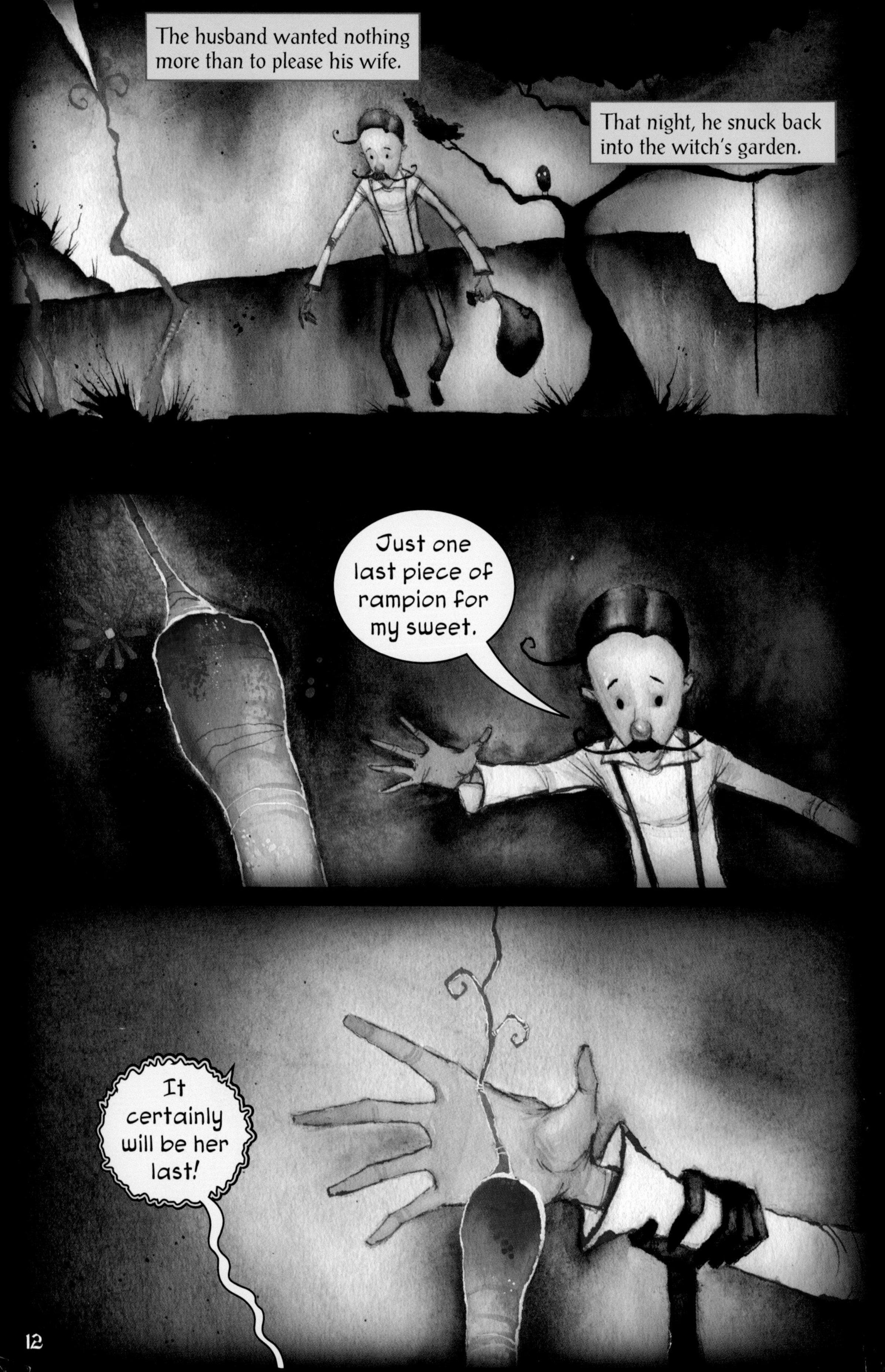
The husband wanted nothing more than to please his wife.
That night, he snuck back into the witch's garden.
Just one last piece of rampion for my sweet.
It certainly will be her last!

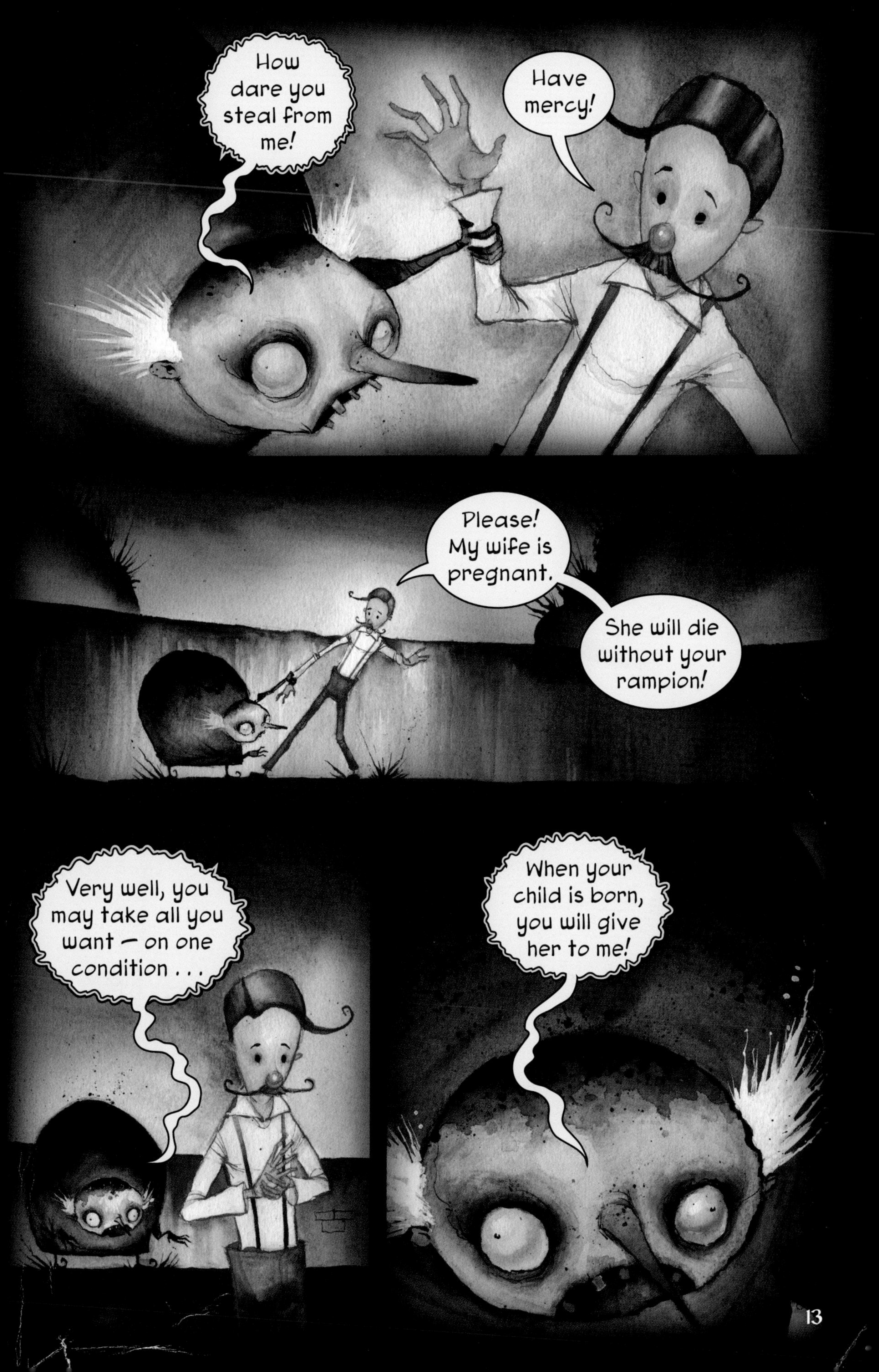
How dare you steal from me!
Have mercy!
Please! My wife is pregnant.
She will die without your rampion!
Very well, you may take all you want — on one condition . . .
When your child is born, you will give her to me!

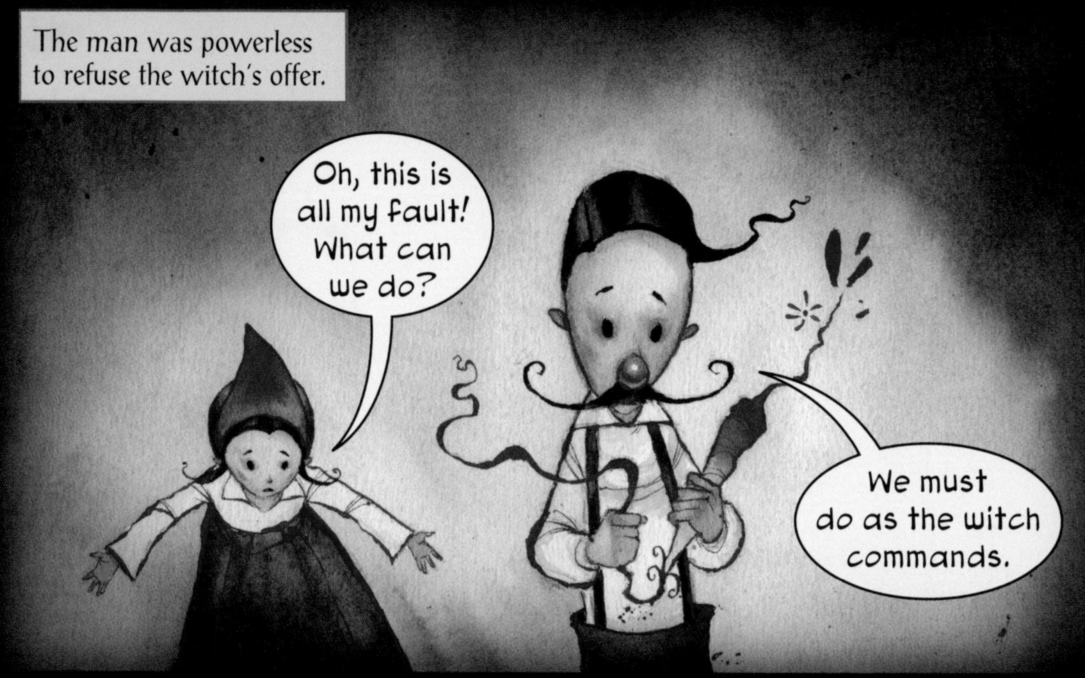
The man was powerless to refuse the witch's offer.
Oh, this is all my fault! What can we do?
We must do as the witch commands.

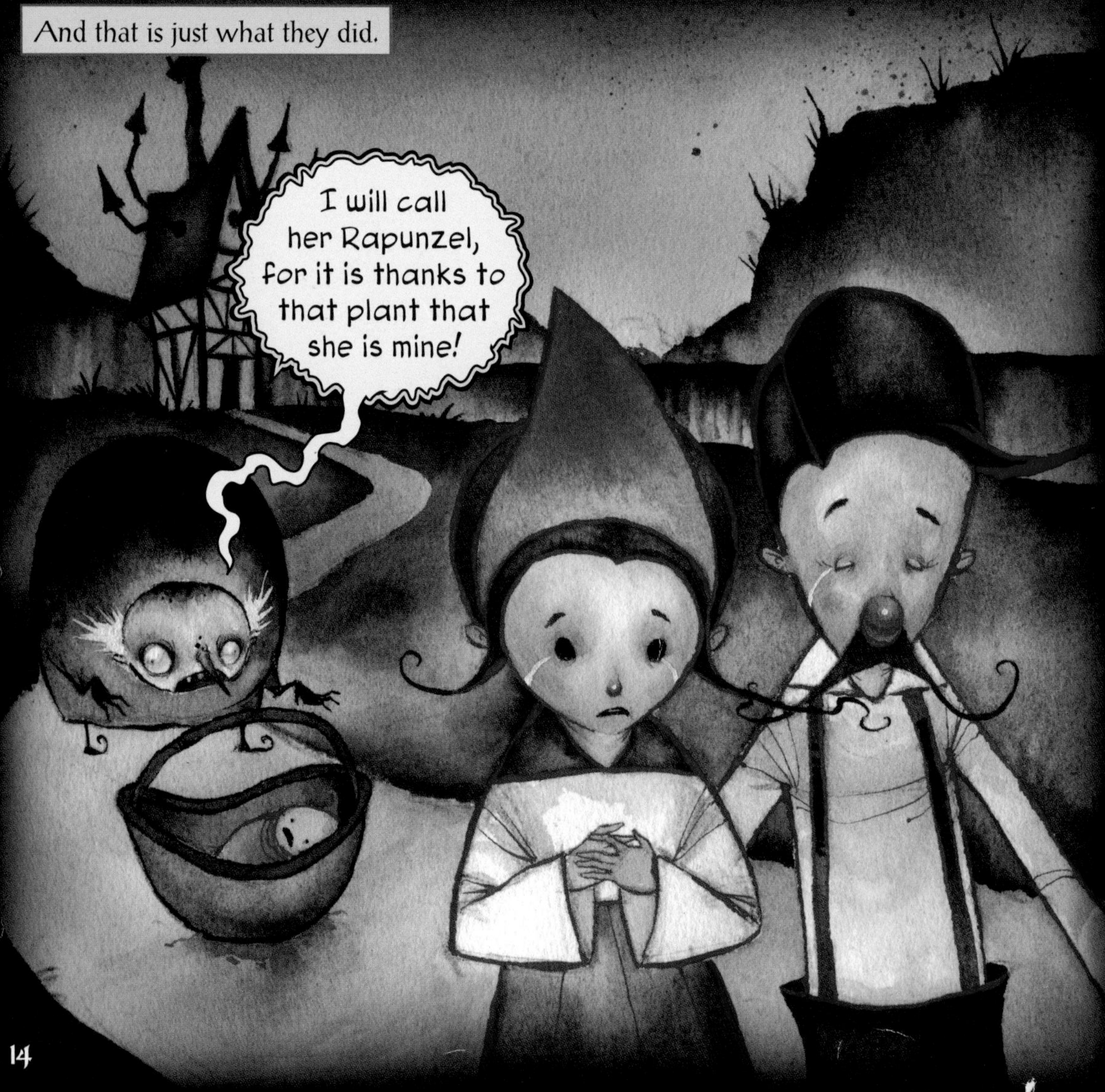
And that is just what they did.
I will call her Rapunzel, for it is thanks to that plant that she is mine!

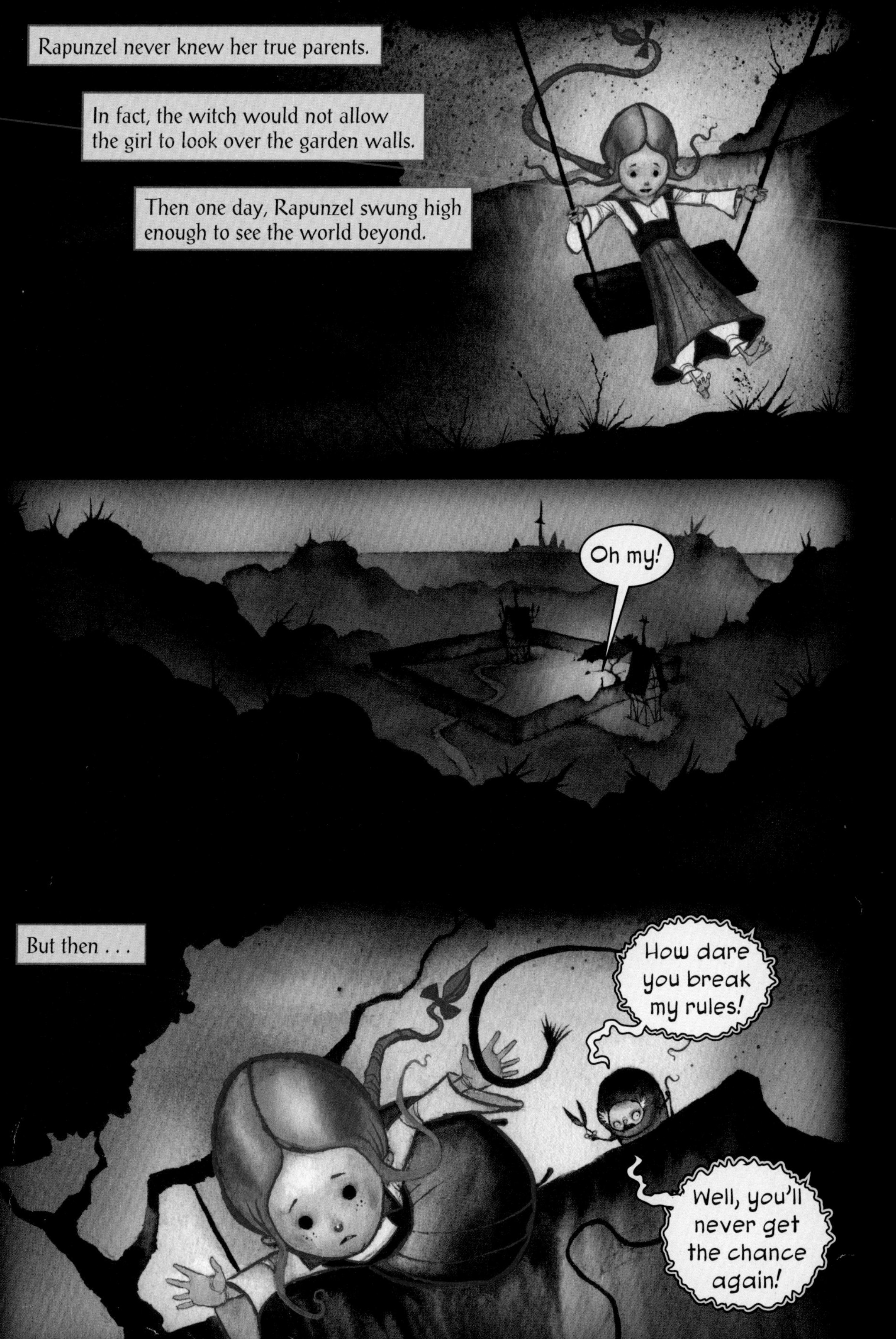
Rapunzel never knew her true parents.
In fact, the witch would not allow the girl to look over the garden walls.
Then one day, Rapunzel swung high enough to see the world beyond.
Oh my!
But then . . .
How dare you break my rules!
Well, you'll never get the chance again!

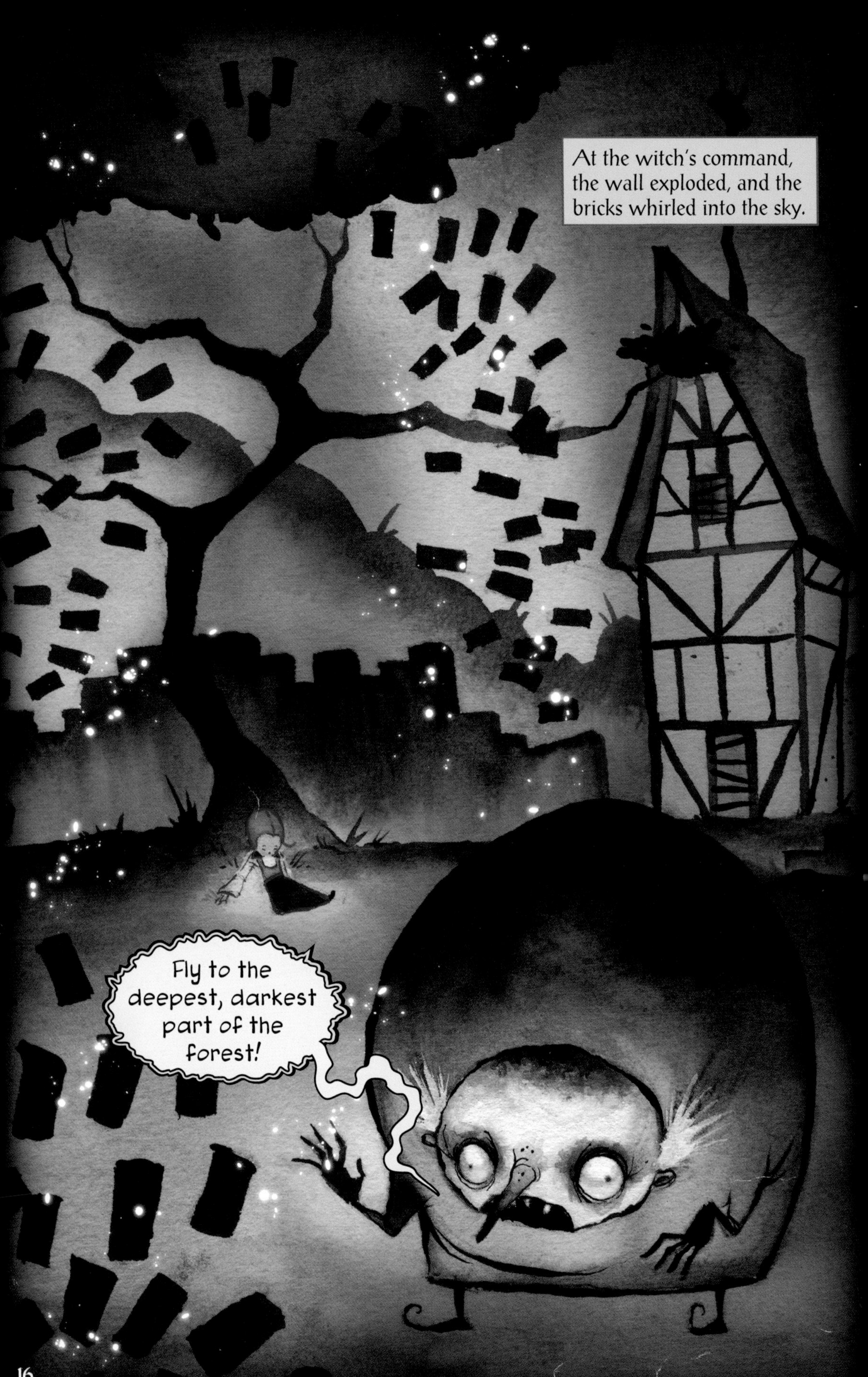
At the witch's command, the wall exploded, and the bricks whirled into the sky.
Fly to the deepest, darkest part of the forest!

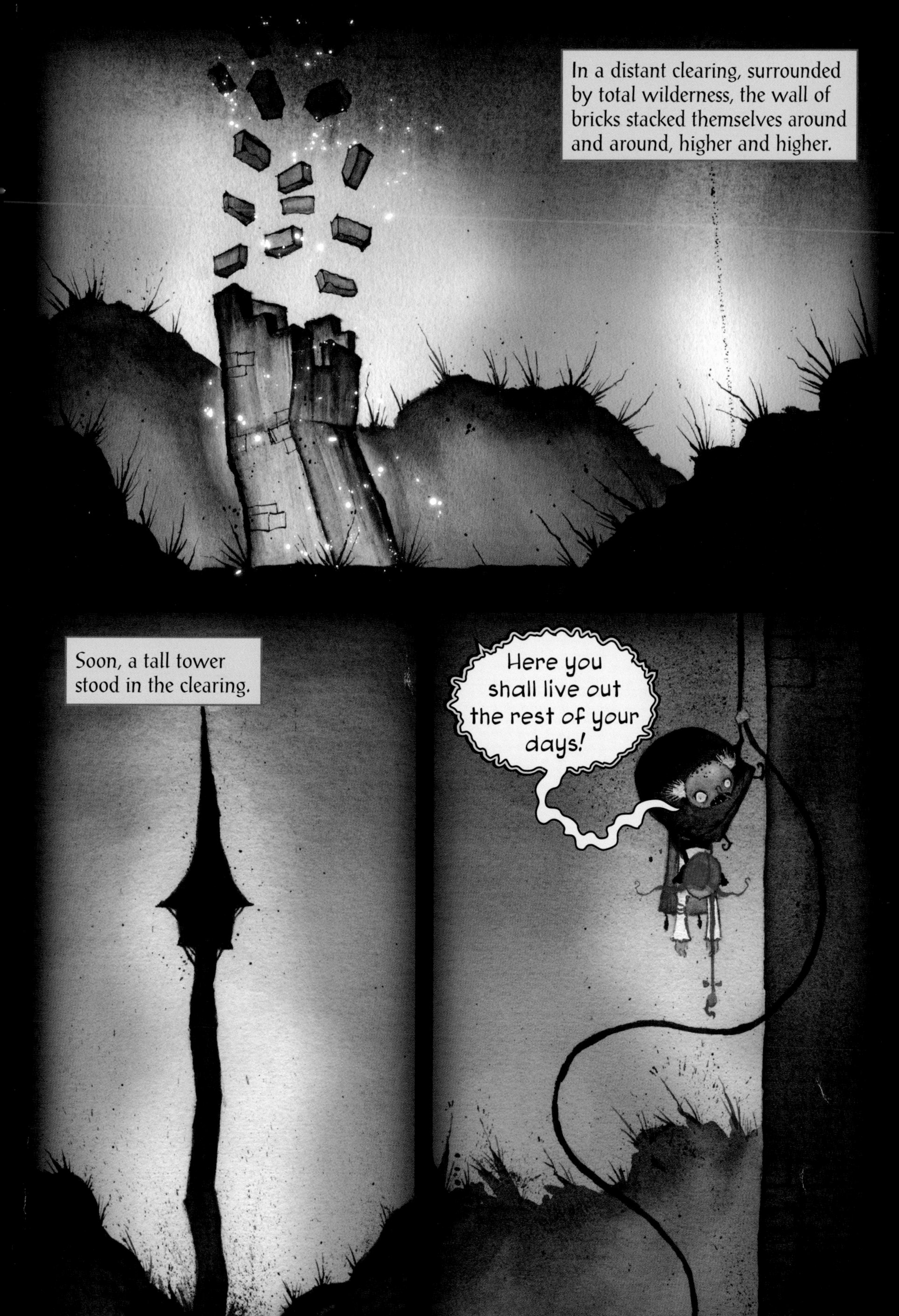
In a distant clearing, surrounded by total wilderness, the wall of bricks stacked themselves around and around, higher and higher.
Soon, a tall tower stood in the clearing.
Here you shall live out the rest of your days!

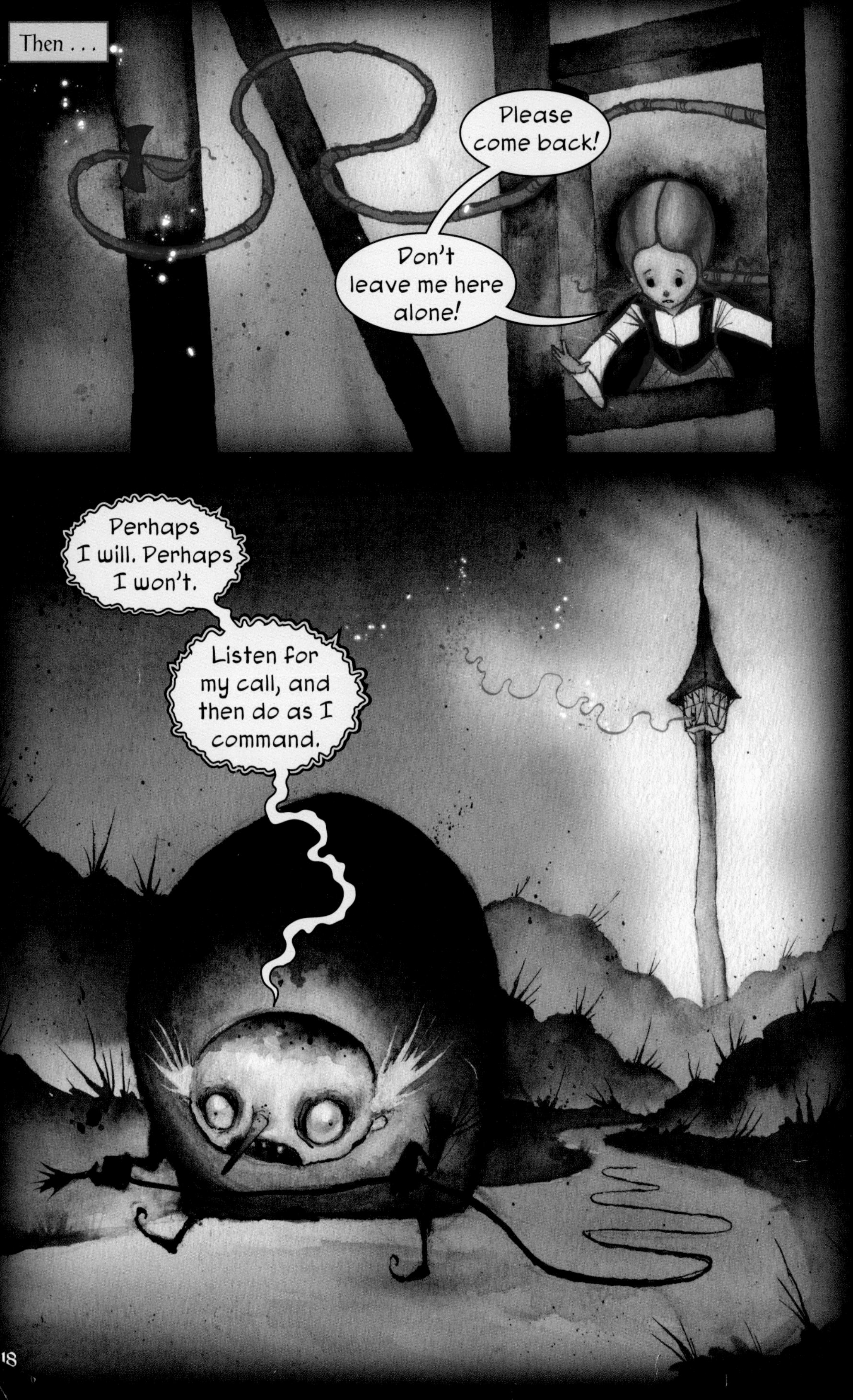
Then . . .
Please come back!
Don't leave me here alone!
Perhaps I will. Perhaps I won't.
Listen for my call, and then do as I command.

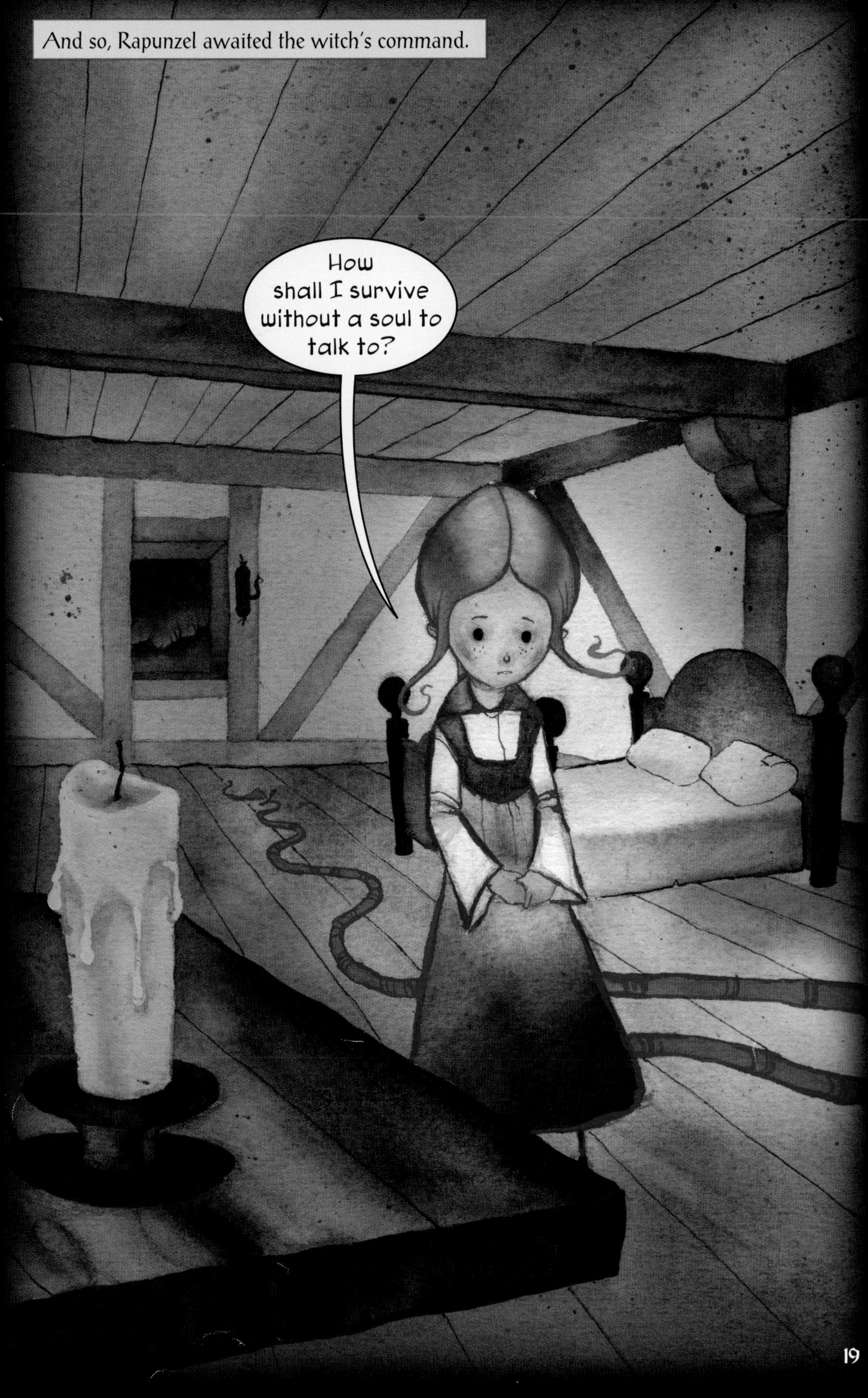
And so, Rapunzel awaited the witch's command.
How shall I survive without a soul to talk to?

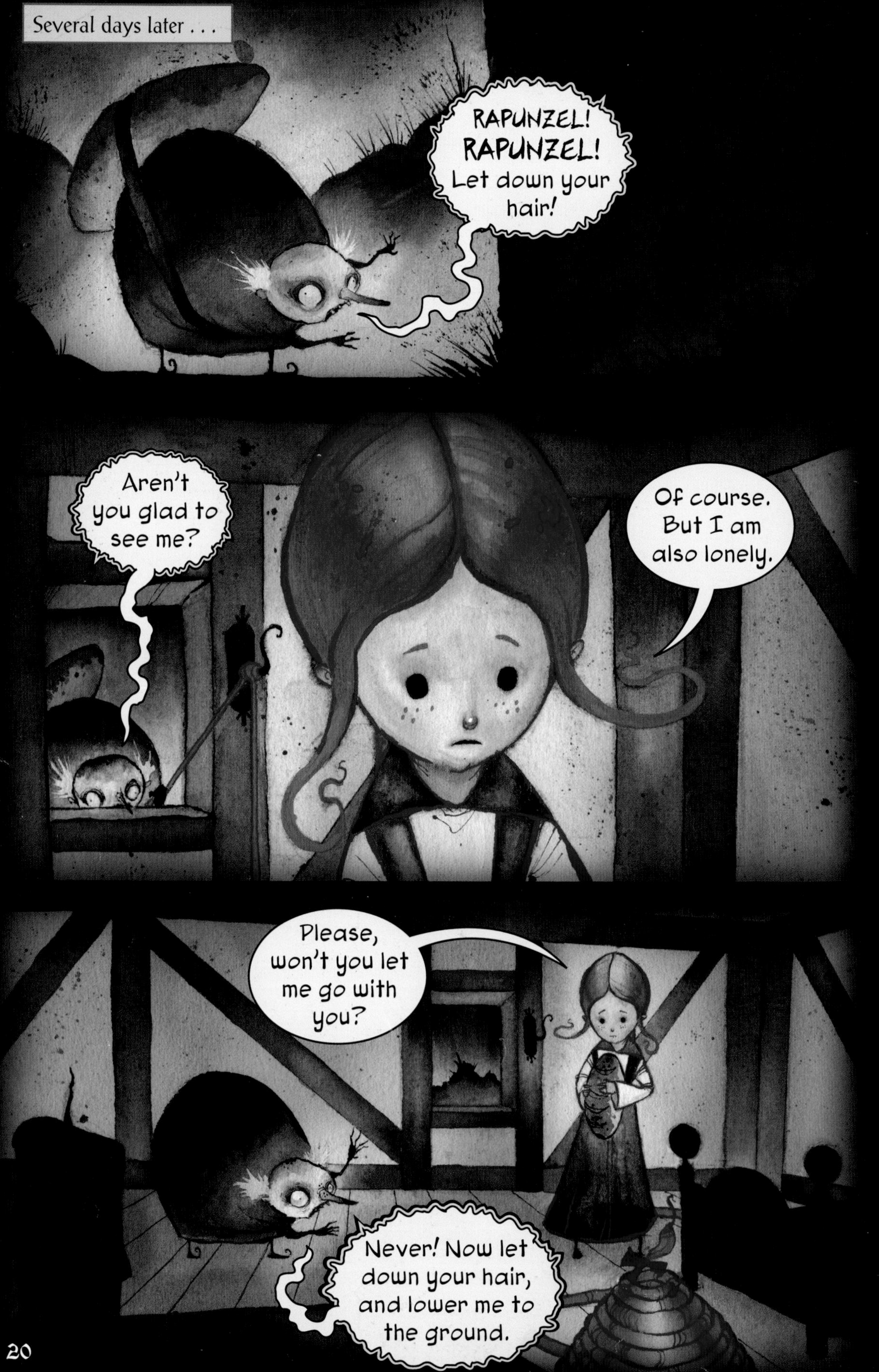
Several days later . . .
RAPUNZEL! RAPUNZEL! Let down your hair!
Aren't you glad to see me?
Of course. But I am also lonely.
Please, won't you let me go with you?
Never! Now let down your hair, and lower me to the ground.

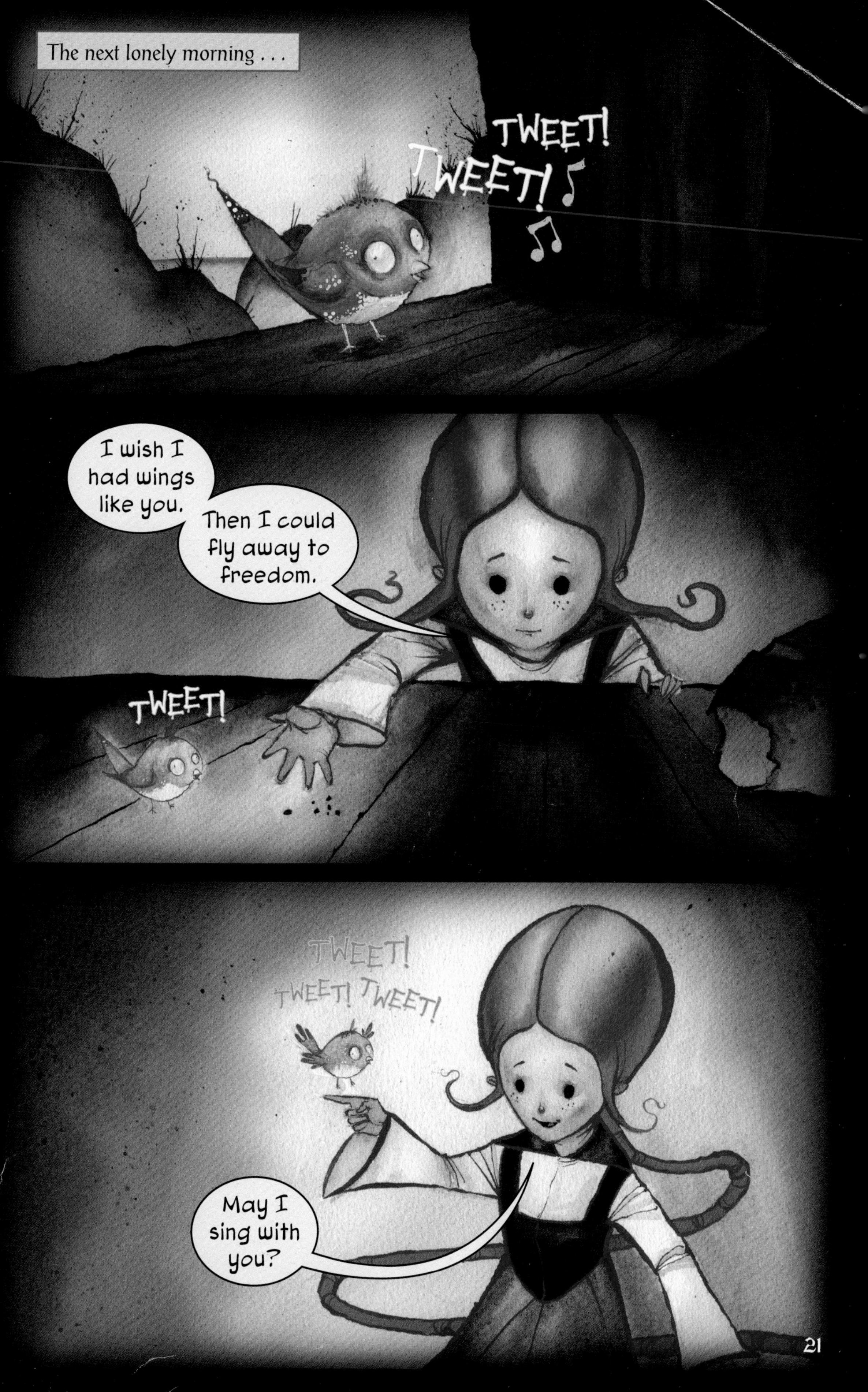

The next lonely morning . . .
TWEET!
TWEET!
I wish I had wings like you.
Then I could fly away to freedom.
TWEET!
TWEET!
TWEET! TWEET!
May I sing with you?

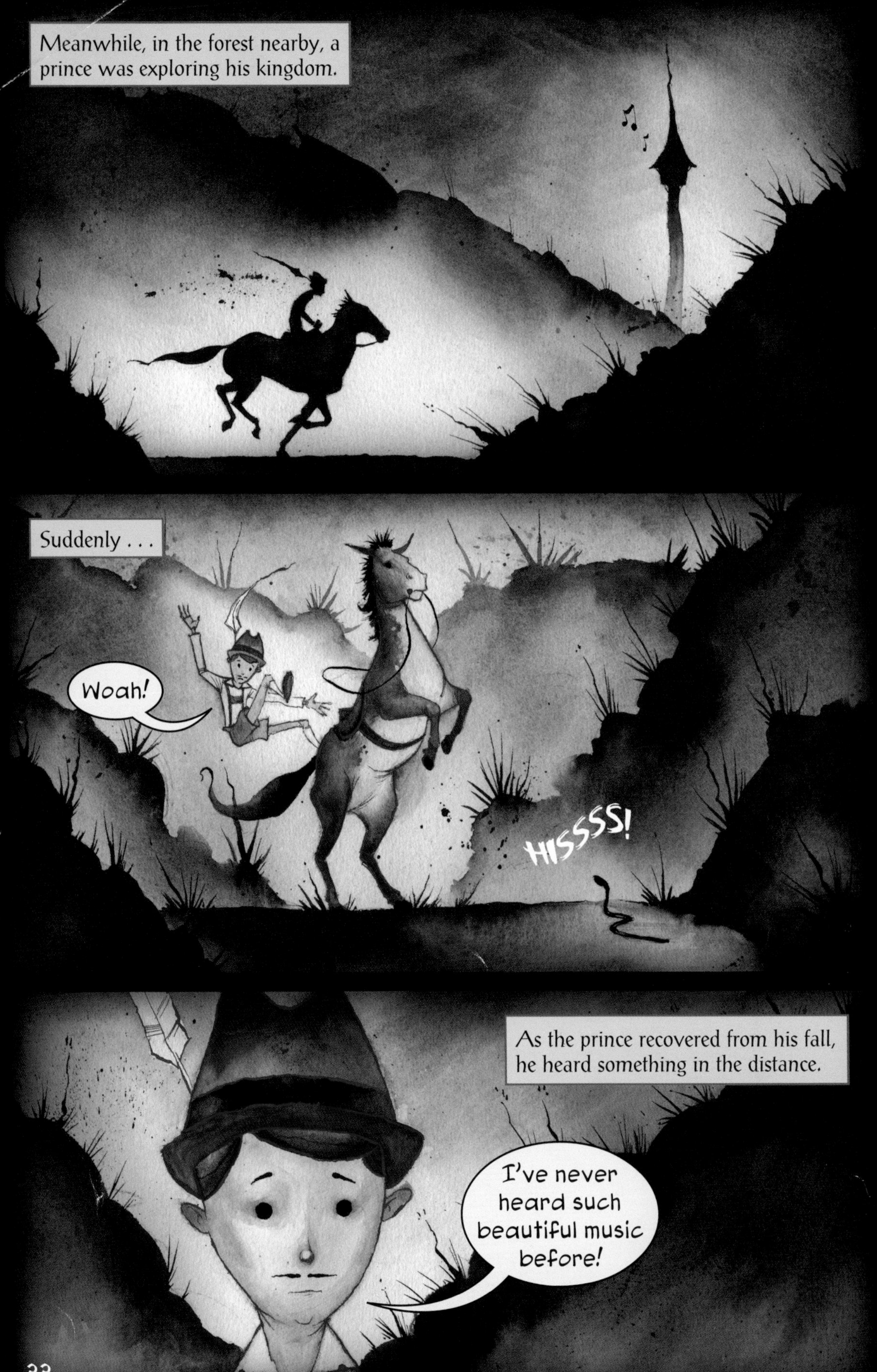
Meanwhile, in the forest nearby, a prince was exploring his kingdom.
Suddenly . . .
Woah!
HISSSS!
As the prince recovered from his fall, he heard something in the distance.
I've never heard such beautiful music before!

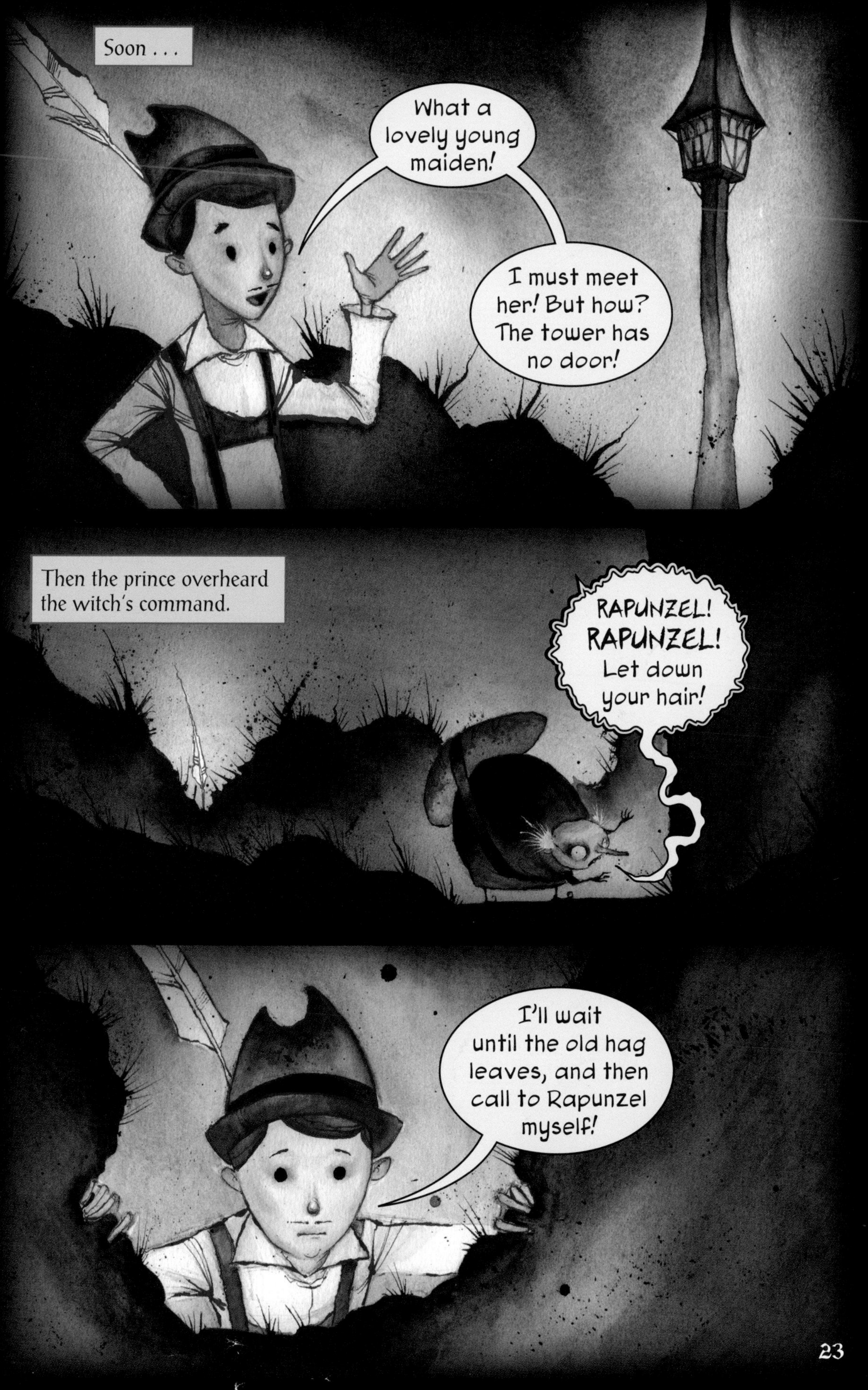
Soon . . .
What a lovely young maiden!
I must meet her! But how? The tower has no door!
Then the prince overheard the witch's command.
RAPUNZEL! RAPUNZEL! Let down your hair!
I'll wait until the old hag leaves, and then call to Rapunzel myself!

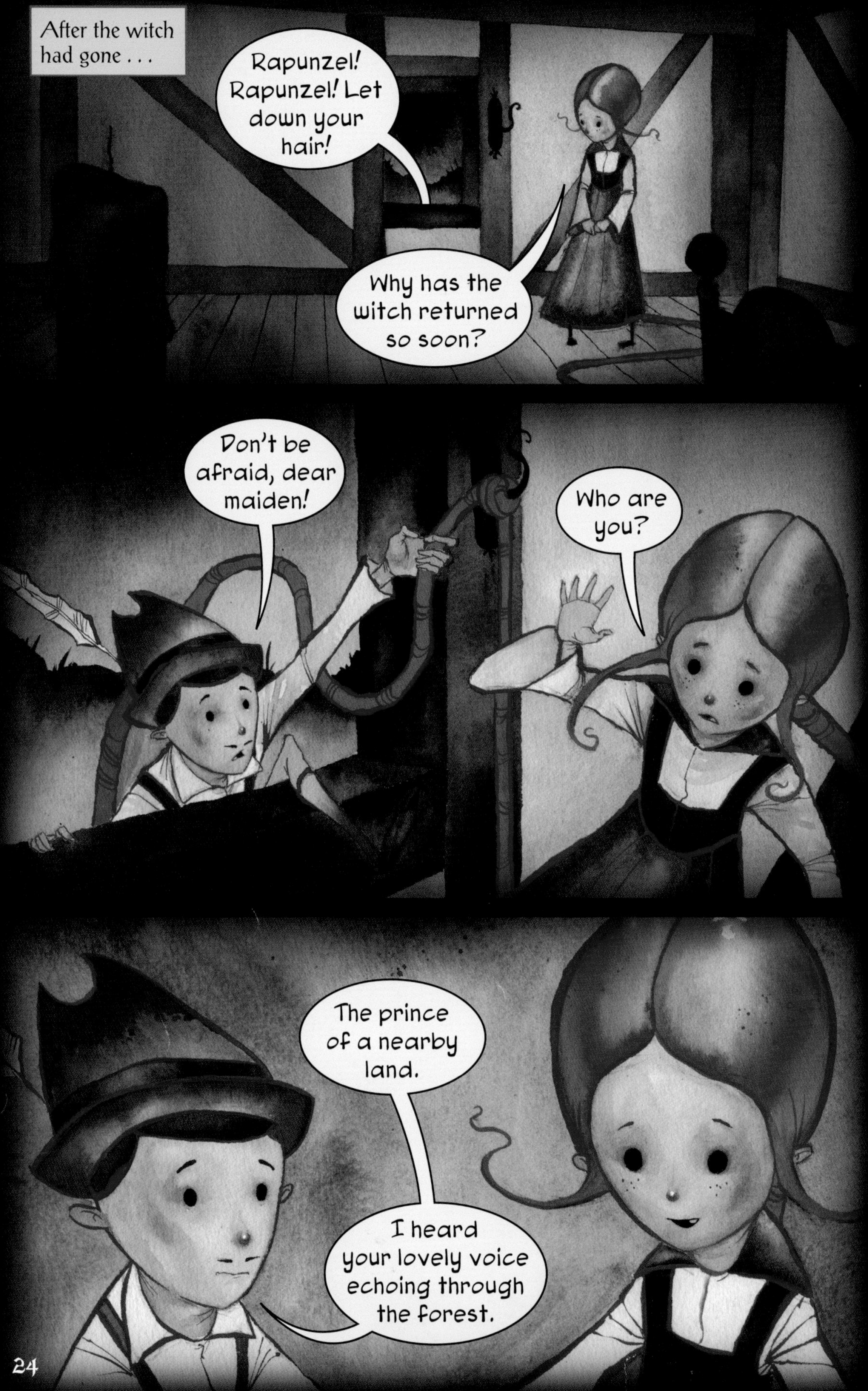
After the witch had gone . . .
Rapunzel! Rapunzel! Let down your hair!
Why has the witch returned so soon?
Don't be afraid, dear maiden!
Who are you?
The prince of a nearby land.
I heard your lovely voice echoing through the forest.

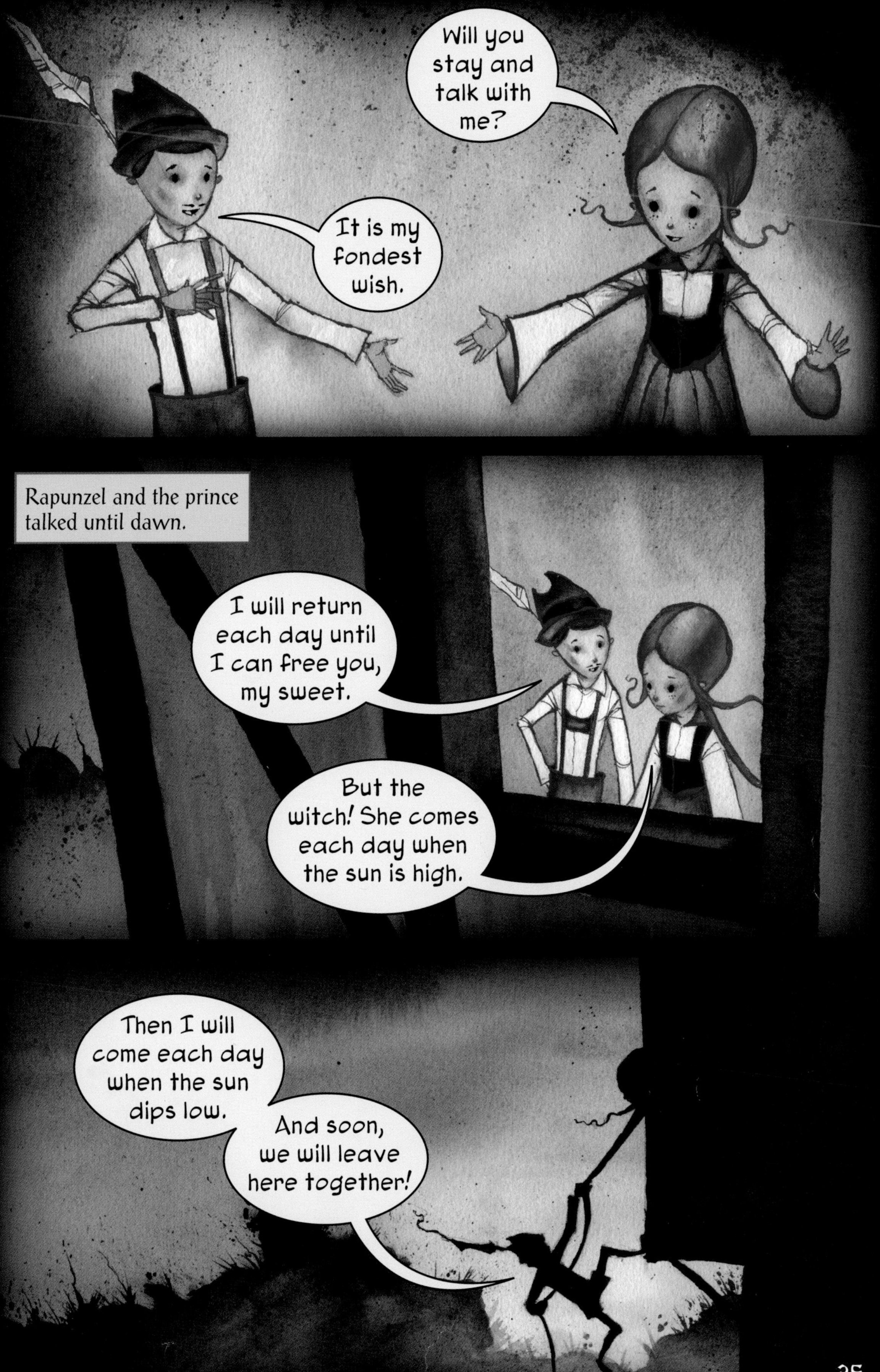
Will you stay and talk with me?
It is my fondest wish.
Rapunzel and the prince talked until dawn.
I will return each day until I can free you, my sweet.
But the witch! She comes each day when the sun is high.
Then I will come each day when the sun dips low.
And soon, we will leave here together!

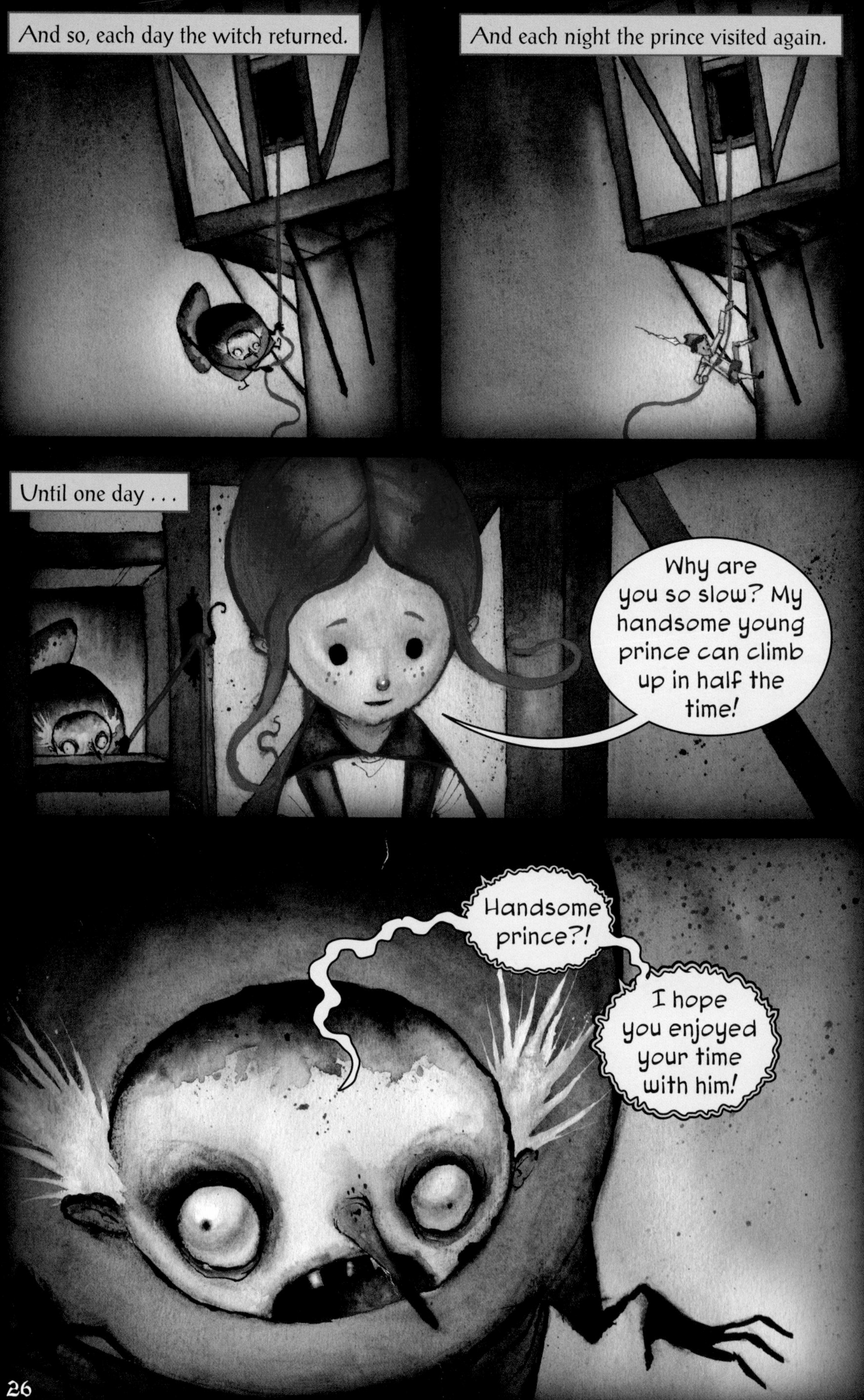
And so, each day the witch returned.
And each night the prince visited again.
Until one day . . .
Why are you so slow? My handsome young prince can climb up in half the time!
Handsome prince?!
I hope you enjoyed your time with him!

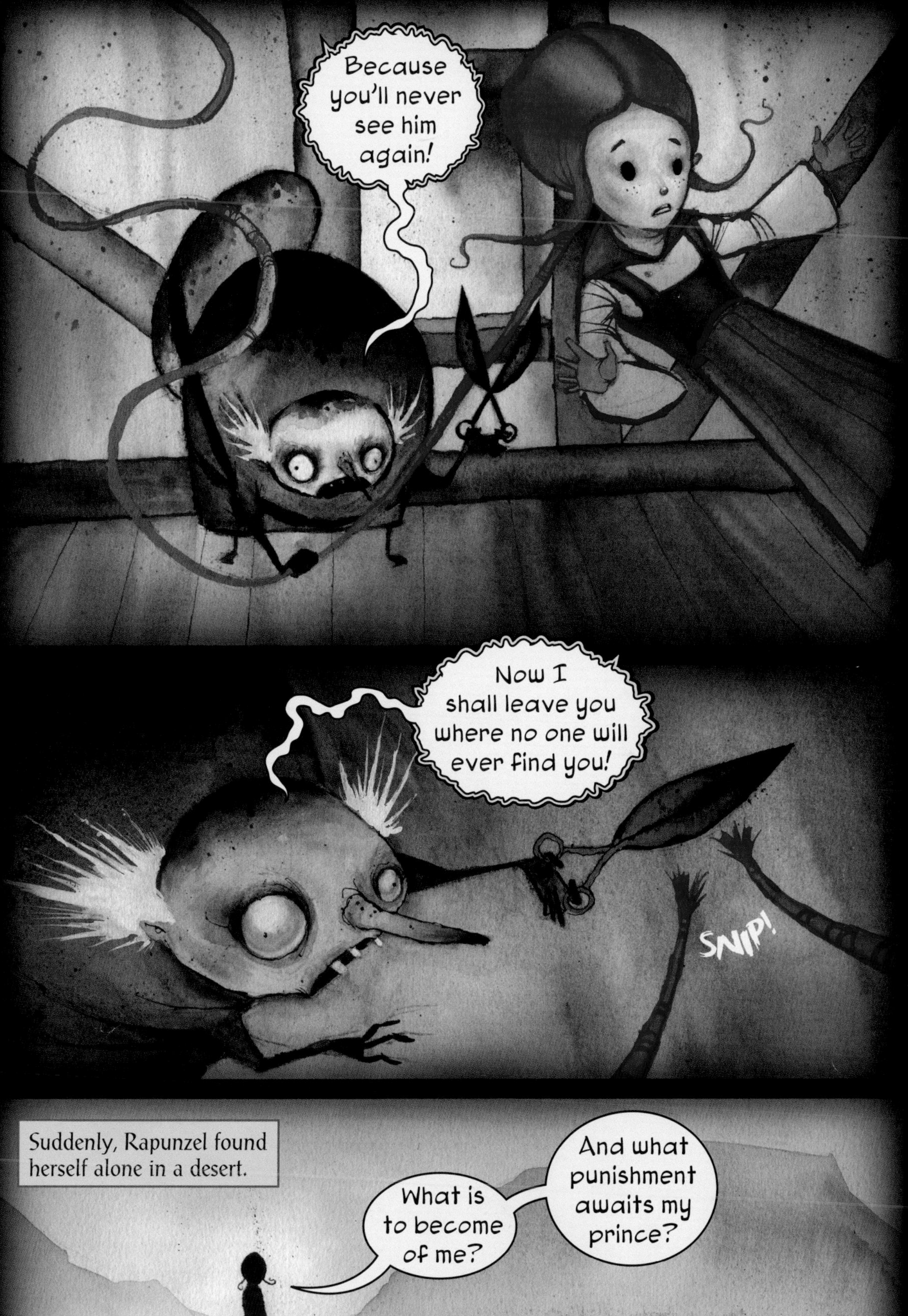
Because you'll never see him again!
Now I shall leave you where no one will ever find you!
SNIP!
Suddenly, Rapunzel found herself alone in a desert.
What is to become of me?
And what punishment awaits my prince?

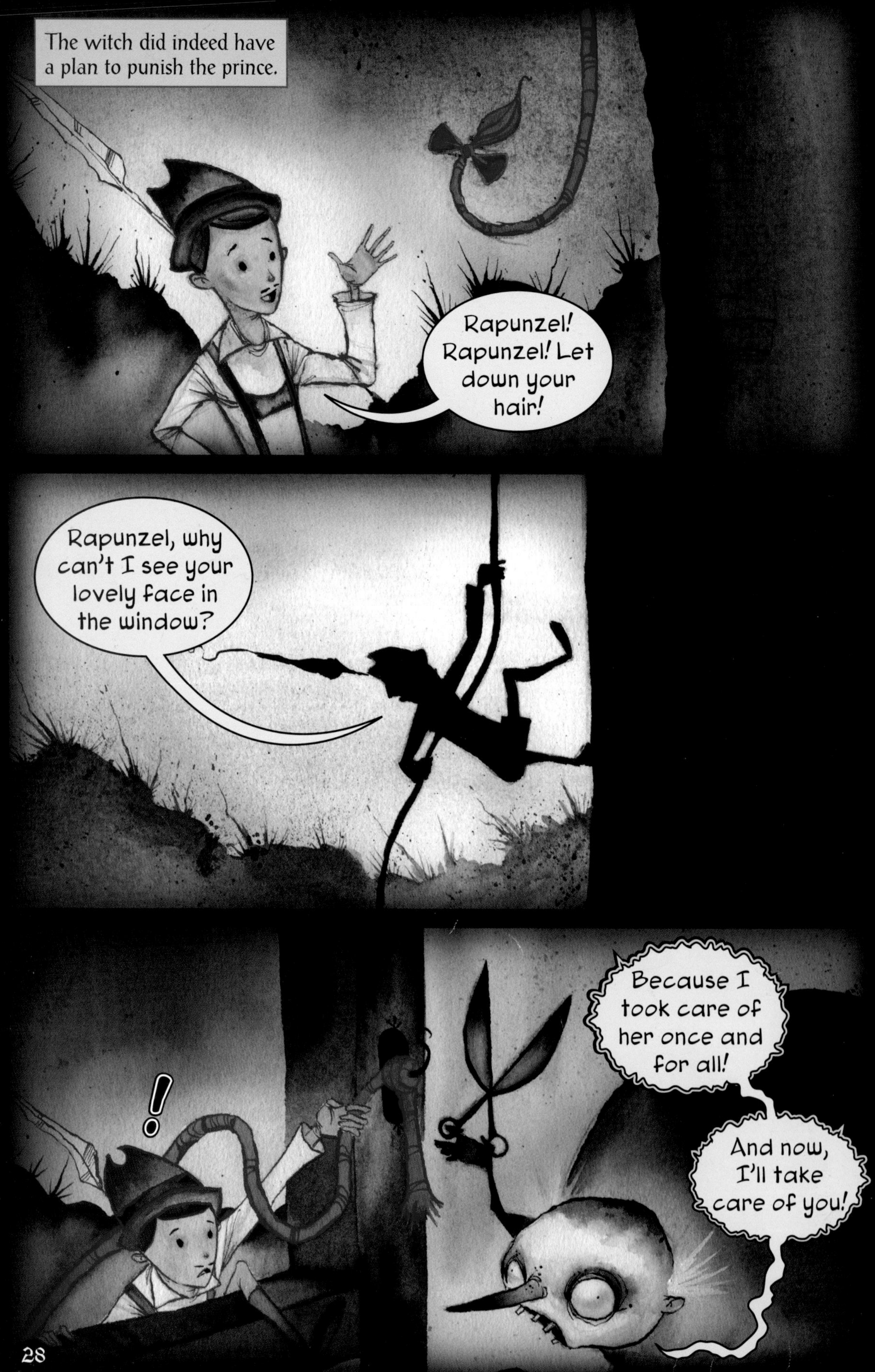
The witch did indeed have a plan to punish the prince.
Rapunzel! Rapunzel! Let down your hair!
Rapunzel, why can't I see your lovely face in the window?
!
Because I took care of her once and for all!
And now, I'll take care of you!

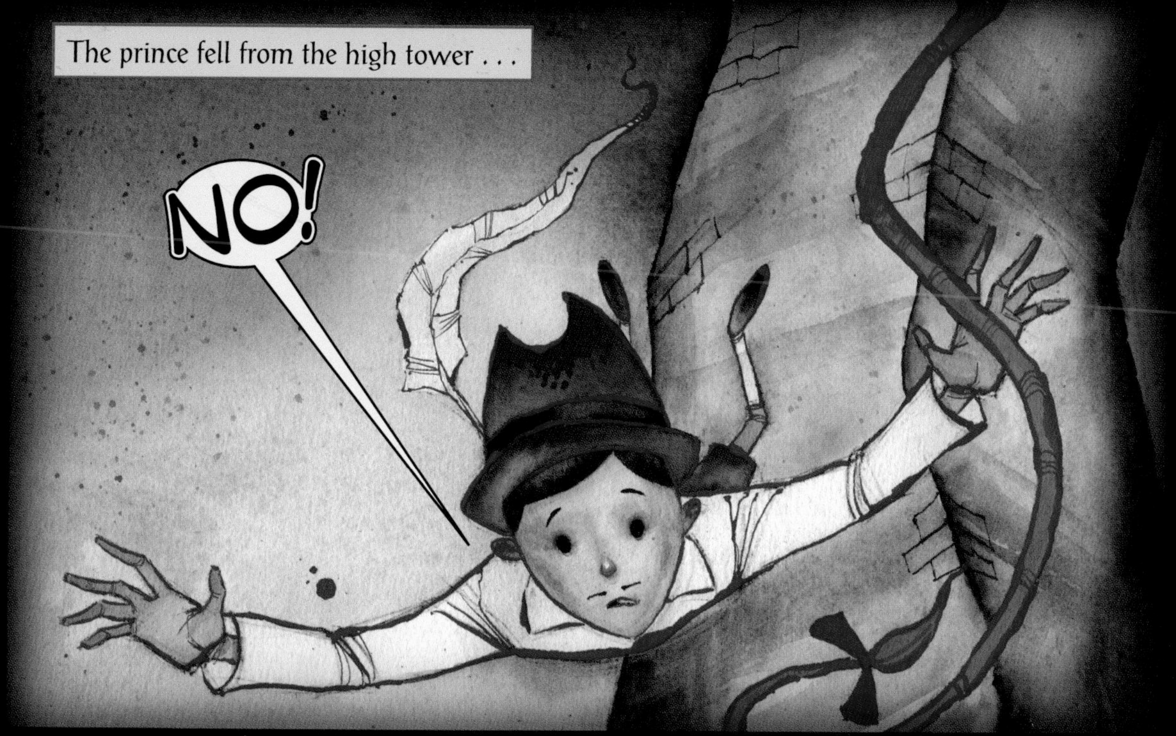
The prince fell from the high tower . . .
NO!

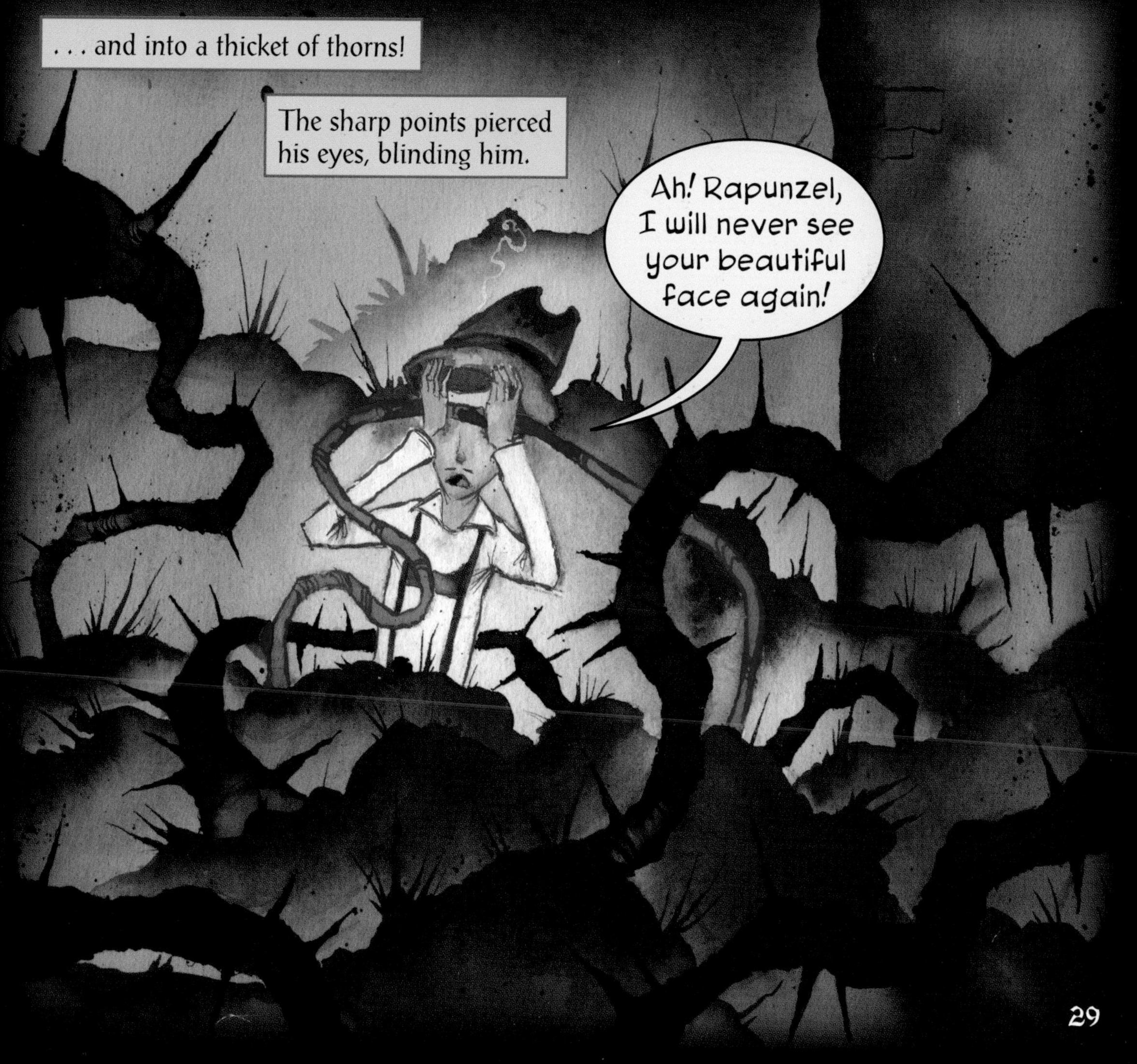
. . . and into a thicket of thorns!
The sharp points pierced his eyes, blinding him.
Ah! Rapunzel, I will never see your beautiful face again!

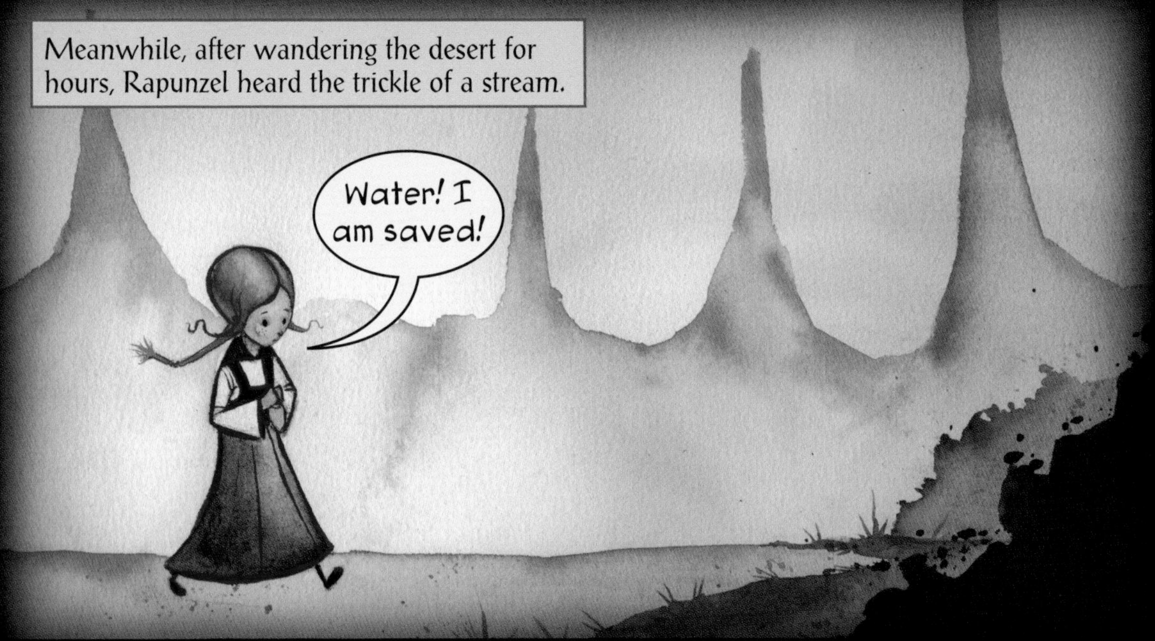
Meanwhile, after wandering the desert for hours, Rapunzel heard the trickle of a stream.
Water! I am saved!

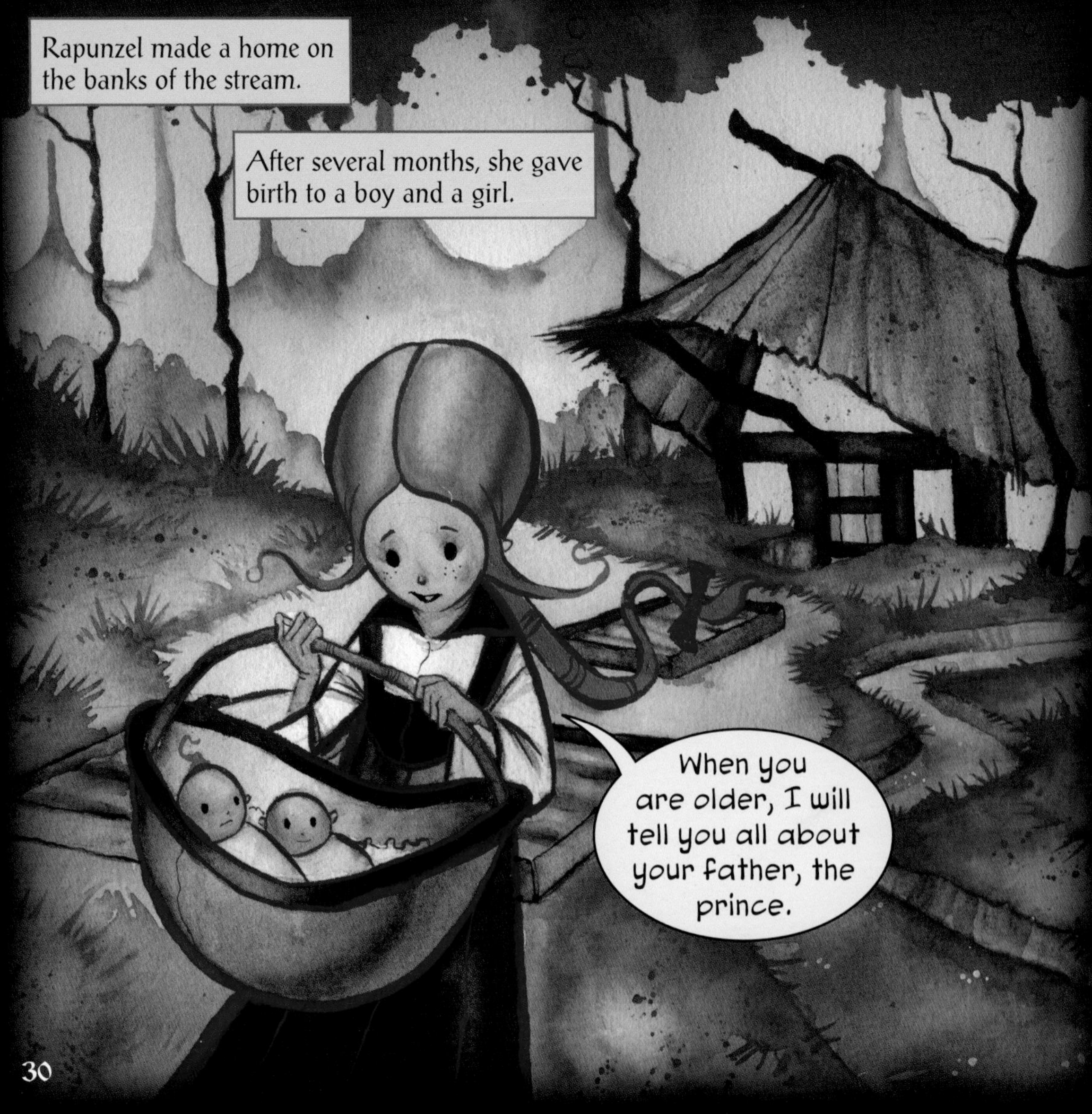
Rapunzel made a home on the banks of the stream.
After several months, she gave birth to a boy and a girl.
When you are older, I will tell you all about your father, the prince.

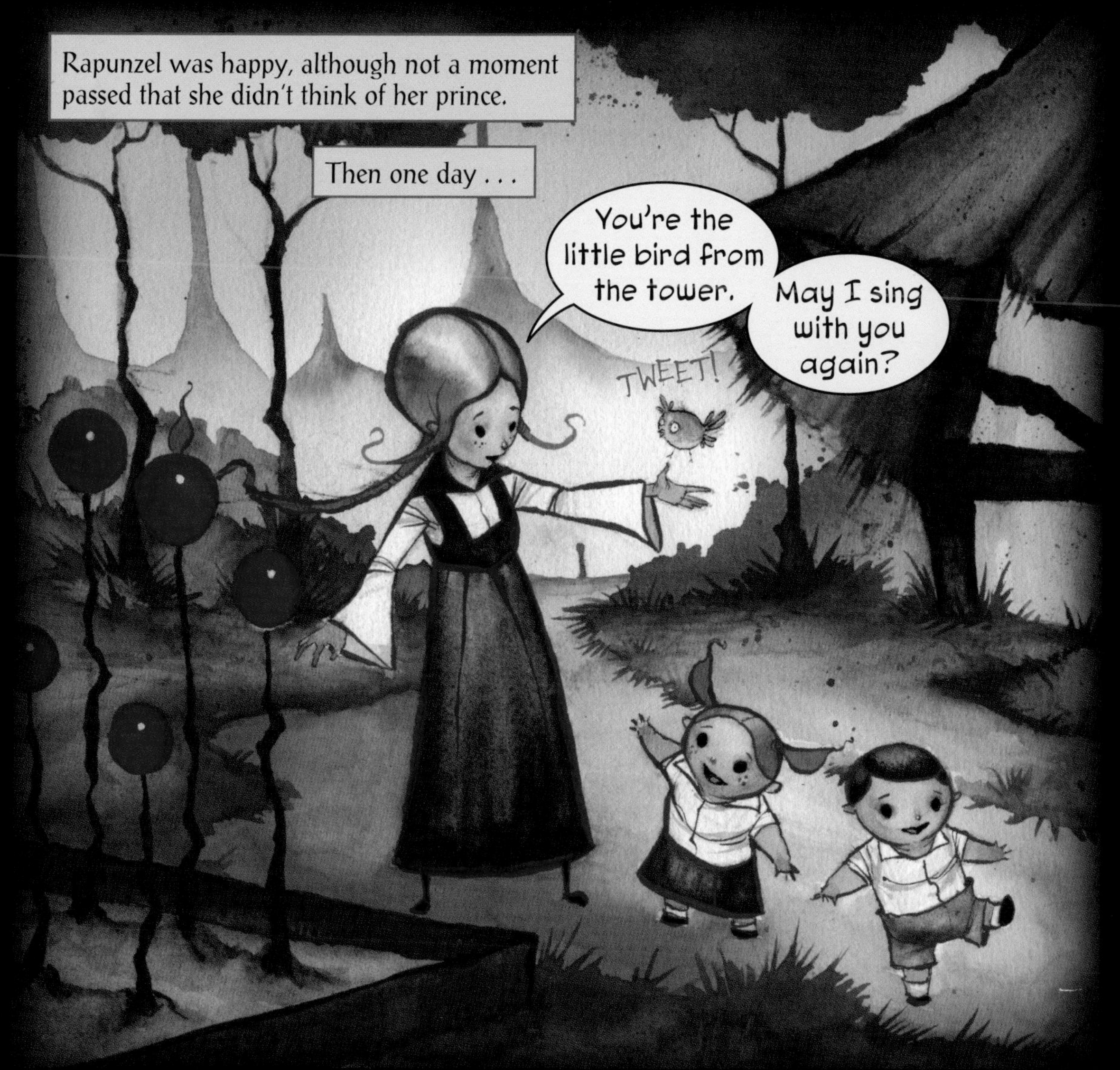
Rapunzel was happy, although not a moment passed that she didn't think of her prince.
Then one day . . .
You're the little bird from the tower.
May I sing with you again?
TWEET!

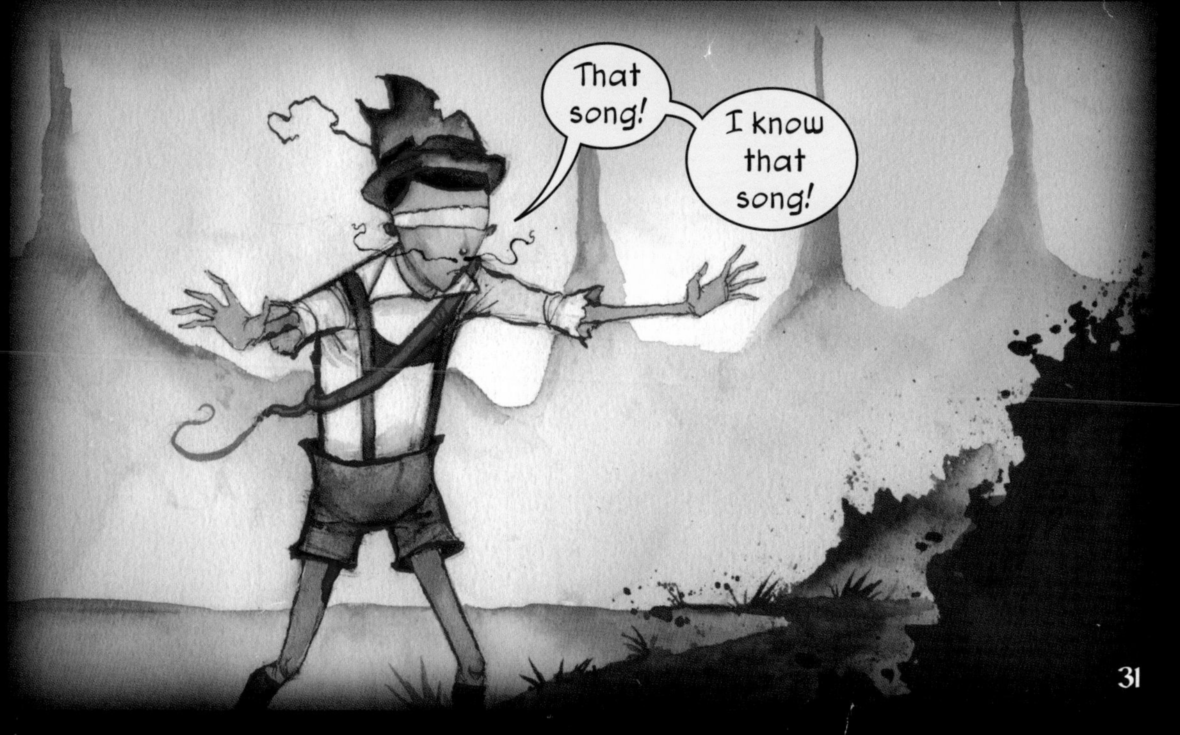
That song!
I know that song!

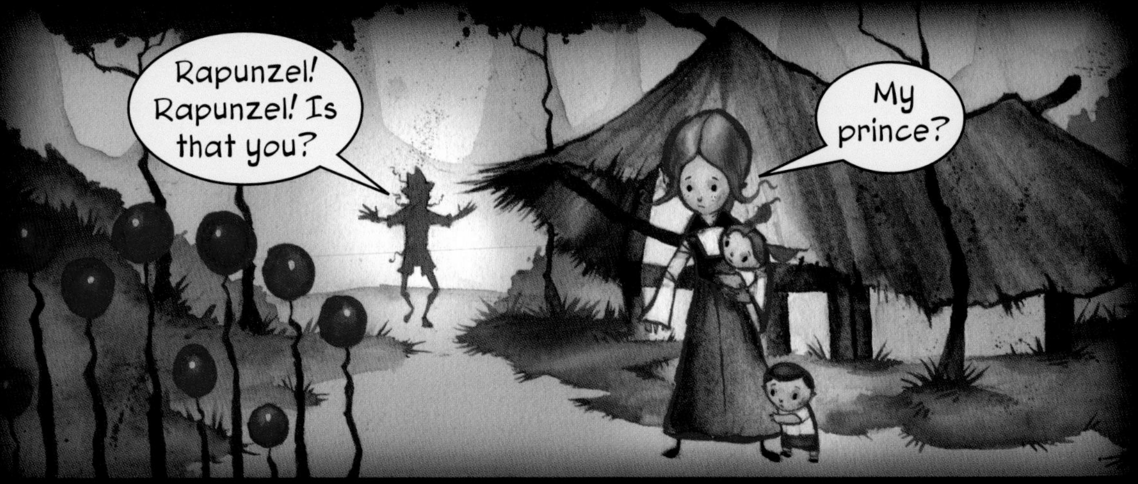
Rapunzel! Rapunzel! Is that you?
My prince?

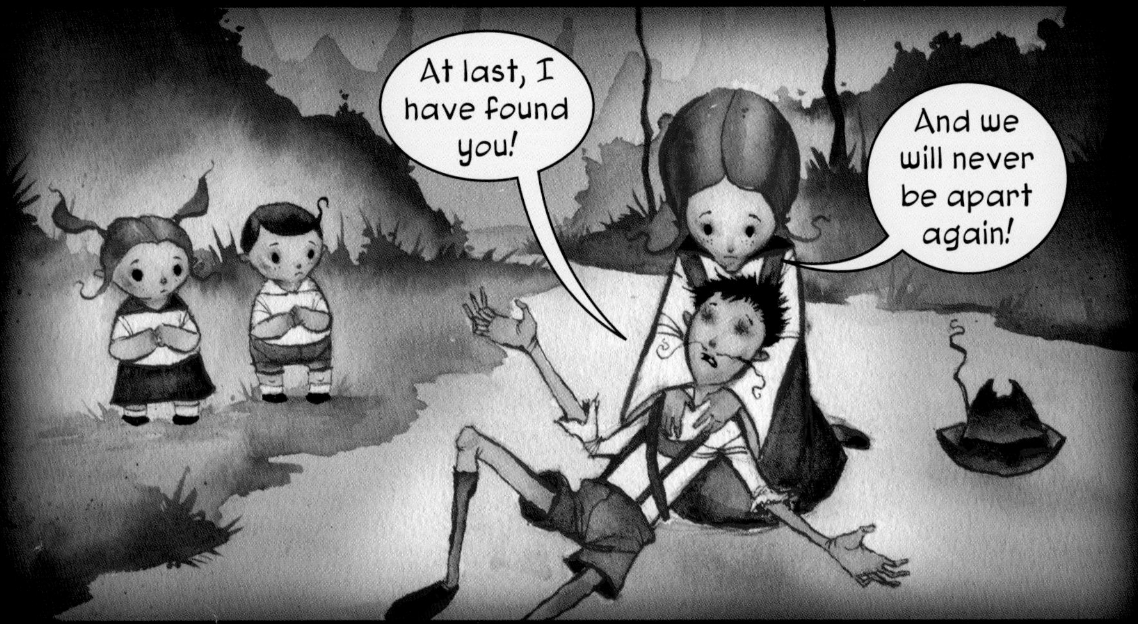
At last, I have found you!
And we will never be apart again!

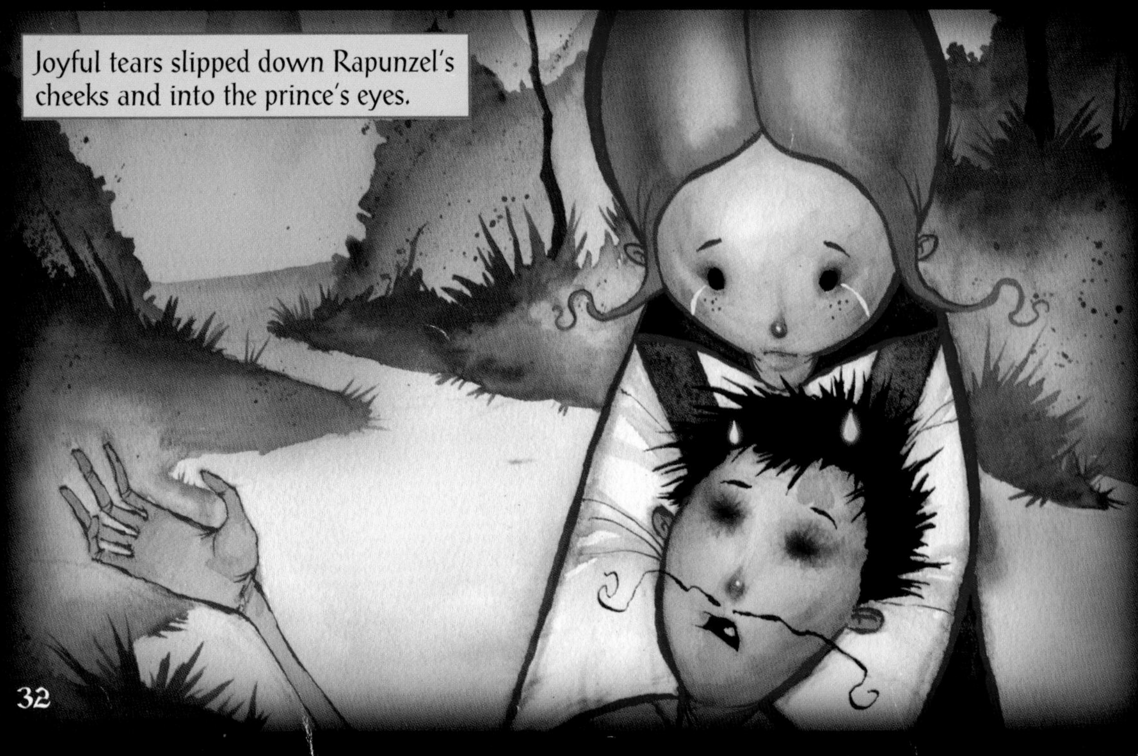
Joyful tears slipped down Rapunzel's cheeks and into the prince's eyes.

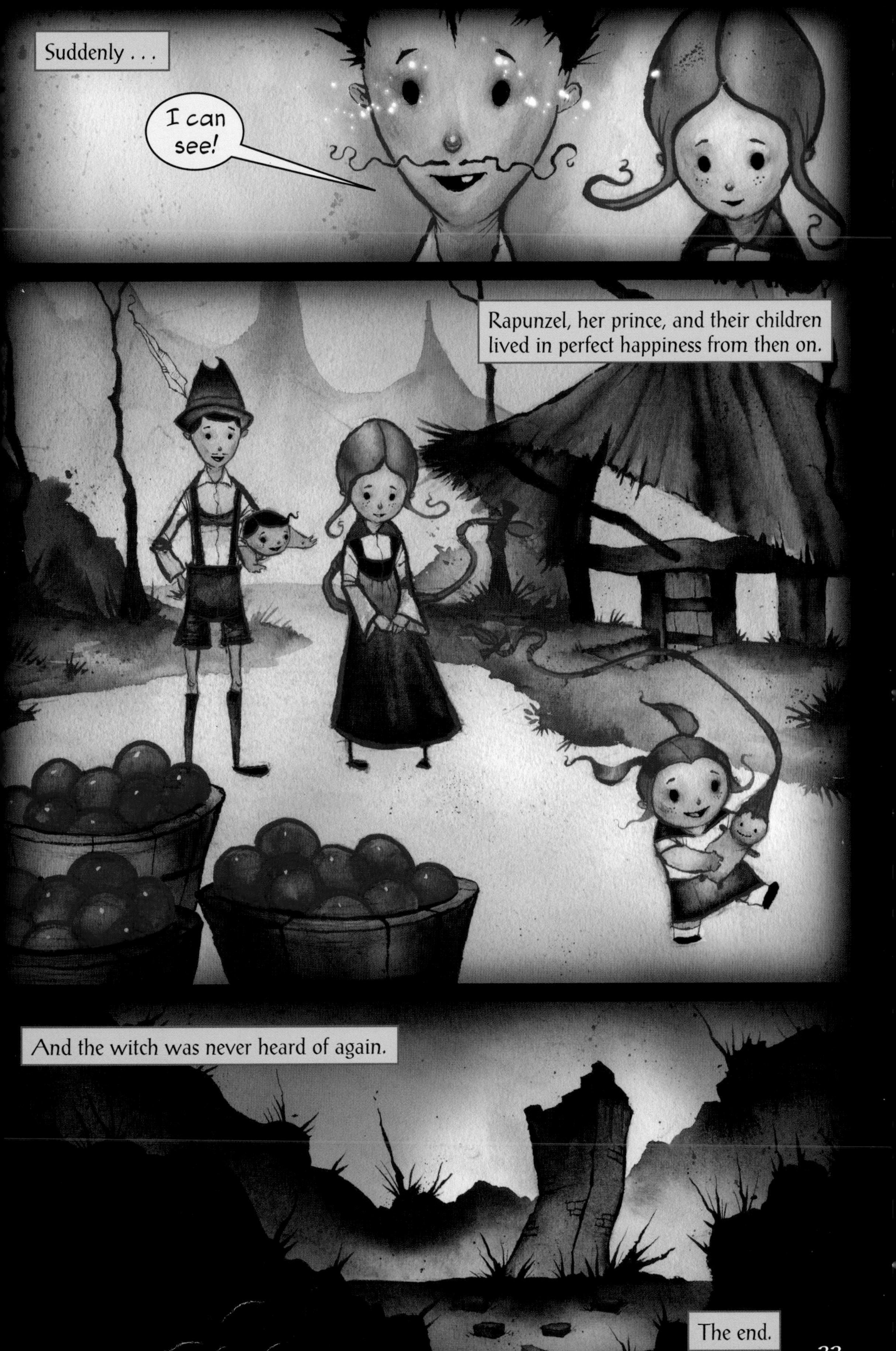

Suddenly . . .
I can see!
Rapunzel, her prince, and their children lived in perfect happiness from then on.
And the witch was never heard of again.
The end.

About the Author

After working more than 10 years as a children's book editor, Stephanie True Peters started writing books herself. She has since written 40 books, including the *New York Times* best seller *A Princess Primer: A Fairy Godmother's Guide to Being a Princess.* When not at her computer, Peters enjoys playing with her two children, hitting the gym, or working on home improvement projects with her patient and supportive husband, Daniel.

About the Illustrator

Jeffrey Stewart Timmins was born July 2, 1979. In 2003, he graduated from the Classical Animation program at Sheridan College in Oakville, Ontario. He currently works as a freelance designer and animator. Even as an adult, Timmins still holds onto a few important items from his childhood, such as his rubber boots, cape, and lensless sunglasses.

Glossary

condition (kuhn-DISH-uhn)—something that needs to happen before another thing can be allowed

dawn (DAWN)—sunrise

fondest (FOND-ist)—most important or most wanted

longing (LAWNG-ing)—wanting something very much

staggered (STAG-urd)—walk shakily or unsteadily

thicket (THIK-it)—a thick growth of plants, bushes, or small trees

wilderness (WIL-dur-niss)—wild land where no one lives

the history of
Rapunzel

Rapunzel and her beautiful hair have been around for centuries. Italian Giambattista Basile wrote down a similar tale called "Petrosinella" in 1637. In this version, the mother-to-be craves *petrosine*, the Italian word for parsley. The witch doesn't separate Petrosinella and her prince. Instead, they run away and marry in secret.

Sixty years later, a French woman, Charlotte Rose de Caumont de la Force, published a collection of fairy tales. A Rapunzel-like story was named "Persinette." *Persille* is the French word for parsley.

Unlike in Basile's version, the couple in the French story do not quickly find a happy ending. The witch continues to make them suffer in the wilderness, even after they have found one another. Finally, though, she realizes she has been wrong. She delivers them to the prince's castle, where Persinette and her family live happily ever after.

"Persinette" was translated into German several times. In one of the German versions the vegetable of choice became rapunzel. Eventually, Jacob and Wilhelm Grimm wrote down the tale. These well-known German brothers recorded many of Europe's folktales and fairy tales. "Rapunzel" is among the most famous of the more than 200 stories the Grimm brothers recorded. And their tale is the most common version told today.

Discussion Questions

1. When Rapunzel was trapped in the tower, she spent most of her days all by herself. Imagine you were trapped by yourself somewhere. How would you spend your time?

2. Each page of a graphic novel has several illustrations called panels. What is your favorite panel in this book? Describe what you like about the illustration and why it's your favorite.

3. Fairy tales are often told over and over again. Have you heard the "Rapunzel" fairy tale before? How is this version of the story different from other versions you've heard, seen, or read?

Writing Prompts

1. Write a new middle and ending for the Rapunzel story. Imagine that her parents had refused to give the witch their baby. What would happen? Would they have to go into hiding? Would the witch catch them and put all three in the tower?

2. Before the prince found Rapunzel in the desert, he was forced to survive on his own. As a blind person in the wilderness, what do you think was the biggest challenge he faced?

3. The story says Rapunzel and her family "lived in perfect happiness from then on." Write a story about their life together. Will they stay in their cottage? Will they try to return to the prince's kingdom?

Internet Sites

The book may be over, but the adventure is just beginning.

Do you want to read more about the subjects or ideas in this book? Want to play cool games or watch videos about the authors who write these books? Then go to FactHound. At *www.facthound.com*, you'll be able to do all that, and more. The FactHound website can also send you to other safe Internet sites.

Check it out!